The Secret Keeper

The Secret Keeper

by
GLORIA WHELAN

ALFRED A. KNOPF
NEW YORK

For Mary Lee Nicholson

This is a Borzoi Book
Published by Alfred A. Knopf, Inc.

Copyright © 1990 by Gloria Whelan
Jacket illustration copyright © 1990 by Maria Jiménez
All rights reserved under International and Pan-American Copyright
Conventions. Published in the United States by Alfred A. Knopf, Inc.,
New York, and simultaneously in Canada by Random House of Canada.
Limited, Toronto. Distributed by Random House, Inc., New York.
Manufactured in the United States of America
Book design by Elizabeth Hardie

2 4 6 8 0 9 7 5 3 1

Library of Congress Cataloging-in-Publication Data
Whelan, Gloria. The secret keeper / by Gloria Whelan. p. cm.
Summary: Sixteen-year-old Annie comes face to face with murder
and kidnapping during what promised to be a
pleasant summer on Lake Michigan.
ISBN 0-679-80572-9 (trade); 0-679-90572-3 (lib. bdg.)
[1. Murder—Fiction.   2. Kidnapping—Fiction.]
I. Title. PZ7.W5718Ke 1990   89-39125 CIP AC

The Secret Keeper

I

$\mathcal{S}$eeing the Beaches for the first time in three years, I am startled by the change. Everything is at risk. The fence that once safeguarded the property is sagging and there are places where it has been pulled down. Lake Michigan has risen and the boardwalk that connects the cabins—not cabins, really, but log mansions with dozens of rooms—is under water. To the west of the cabins the sand dunes have inched closer, like great humped beasts shifting in their sleep, sifting sand over the porches and yards. The wild wood lilies and orange butterfly weed, the asters and thistles and windflowers, have nudged out the rose gardens and flower beds where impatiens and begonias once bloomed.

I have come back after reading in the newspaper that the members of the Beaches have made a gift of their property to the state. It's to be a park. Those years when only a privileged few could enjoy the hundreds of acres of beach and woods are over. The cabins will be torn down. The article suggested that the encroachment of the lake and the dunes had discouraged the club members. But for me the Beaches came to an end three years ago, the summer I was Matt's keeper.

The Beaches is in the northern part of the state. The Larimers had brought me there to be a keeper for their grandson. I had already worked that past winter as a baby-sitter for the Larimers in the suburb of Colonial Gardens. Matt, who was ten, had hooded gray eyes and brown hair that fell over his forehead. He was small for his age and seemed to be lost in the Larimers' huge home. He was quiet, but he didn't miss anything, watching you whenever he thought you weren't looking at him. He nibbled endlessly on his nails, as if he had some perpetual quarrel with them.

I got along well with Matt because we had something in common. He had lost his mother and I had lost my father. Matt's mother had died the previous fall. My father hadn't died, but he and my mom had gotten a divorce, and he was a couple of thousand miles away and hardly ever wrote to me.

I know divorce happens to a lot of people, but knowing that doesn't help when it happens to you. I guess my parents had their reasons, but they didn't discuss them with me. My mom said, "Annie, your dad and I don't want to say anything negative about each other." I wasn't supposed to notice the doors slamming or the hateful whispers or the expensive-looking envelopes with engraved return addresses from their attorneys. Mom had gone back to work so we could keep our house in Colonial Gardens. She was tired all the time and cried a lot when she thought I didn't notice. I felt sorry for her, but deep down I was relieved to be escaping to the Beaches.

Mrs. Larimer is a descendant of Hawkins Bradford, the founder of the Beaches. Both she and her husband had been summering at the Beaches all their lives, just as their parents and grandparents had before them. At the Beaches every child had to have a keeper. The members were afraid their children might drown or get lost in the woods, and then there were cocktail parties and tennis competitions where no one wanted little children around. But with the Larimers it was something else.

At first all I knew was that in the fall Matt's mother, Jess, had died unexpectedly and that his father, Bryce, didn't seem to be around. But early in June, two weeks before we left for the Beaches, Mrs. Larimer asked me over, not to baby-sit but just to talk. I was always a little intimidated by the Larimers' home—the grand white colonial with a row of pillars marching across the front, the spacious rooms furnished in elegant antiques, the swaths of silk drapery, and the rugs with their gently faded patterns of scrolls and roses.

I sat on the edge of a large tapestry-covered chair feeling like Alice in Wonderland after she drank the shrinking potion. Mrs. Larimer sat across from me looking as though she hadn't made up her mind until that very minute whether she ought to confide in me. From the pictures I had seen of her, I knew Mrs. Larimer had once been a beautiful woman, but now she looked worn, and you felt when you talked with her that she wasn't quite there. I thought it was because of her daughter's death.

She took a deep breath. "Anne," she said, "I want you to promise me that what I tell you won't go any further. We've asked you to be a keeper for Matt this summer because Mr. Larimer and I trust you." Here she gave me a long, intense look. Perhaps seeing that all this was intimidating, she smiled and reached over to pat me on the arm with a cold hand.

"You might as well hear this from me, Anne. At the Beaches some of the staff and the keepers are from Lakeville, where my daughter lived. I don't say they'll gossip, but if they do, I want you to be able to distinguish fact from rumor.

"Our daughter, Jess, was married to Bryce Stevens. He came from Lakeville, which is a small town near the Beaches. Bryce's father, Len, was a caretaker at the Beaches. Len's dead now." She stopped as if considering whether more might be said about his death but left it at that.

"After their marriage Jess and Bryce settled down near Lakeville in a farmhouse. Jess was something of a romantic and I think she liked the idea of living in an old farmhouse in the country. We sent over a lot of things from our cottage, and she did a wonderful job of fixing up the house. She was always quite artistic.

"It happened last Labor Day weekend. We were at the Beaches. Jess and Matt and her husband were at their home in Lakeville. Her husband"—Mrs. Larimer kept avoiding his name—"didn't like Jess and Matt coming to the Beaches, but I won't go into that. I'll just say their marriage was not an entirely happy one.

"Jess came to see us with Matt on that Sunday evening. We believe there had been an argument with her husband, because she was rather upset—someone might mention that to you. She left Matt with us and started home again. It was dark and raining and the roads were slippery. Shortly after she left the Beaches she had an accident. Thomas, our maintenance man at the Beaches, happened to pass her car and found her." Mrs. Larimer seemed to close an invisible book. She looked up at me, leaving time for questions but clearly not wanting any.

But I couldn't help myself. "Where was her husband?" It was the wrong question for me to ask and the wrong time to ask it. For a moment Mrs. Larimer couldn't hide her impatience with me.

"He was at their house." At first I thought that was all she was going to say, but even to her it must have seemed brusque. "Of course he was beside himself. We all were. These last nine months have been especially awful for Matt."

I could see I wasn't to ask any more questions. "I'm telling you all of this, Anne, so you won't listen to rumors," said Mrs. Larimer. "But there is something else which is more important." I realized that all of the things she had told me were leading to what she would now say. "It's why we chose someone dependable like you to be Matt's keeper. Matt's father has agreed not to see Matt. There was some unpleasantness and it's absolutely crucial for Matt's welfare, almost a matter of life or death—of course I don't mean that literally, only psychologically—that Bryce be kept away from Matt." At last the father's name, I thought. "Even though he's not living in Lakeville now, it was his home and it's close to the Beaches. If you see something at all suspicious you must tell us at once."

I was puzzled. Mrs. Larimer was trying to appear open and candid but although I was sure there was a lot she wasn't telling me, in my eagerness to get to the Beaches I put the conversation out of my mind.

2

$\mathcal{M}$y first few days at the Beaches I walked around wide-eyed—at the huge cabins with their long porches furnished in freshly painted wicker and crowded with pots of bright flowers, at the dazzle of the sun on the great blue lake, the sailboats with their spinnakers in colors as bright as the flowers, and—a wild extravagance in all that sandy soil—the croquet court with its stretch of immaculately cropped lush green grass. I tried not to stare, but I saw that the Larimers were amused by my all too obvious awe.

Matt was less impressed and more wary. While my role was clear—in spite of the rather impressive title of keeper, I was merely a kind of servant—Matt belonged to the Beaches, and the members went out of their way of help Matt feel at home. He was given tennis and sailing lessons, and the parents of the other children invited him over to their cabins. Since I usually went along and there were only a dozen cabins, I quickly got to know everyone.

The Larimers did everything they could to make me feel at home. My room had been freshly papered in a Laura Ashley print with matching linens on the bed. The furniture was turn-of-the-century summer cottage, but it was painted white and decorated with little flowers to match the linens. When I awoke in the morning the reflection of the sun on the lake shimmered on my ceiling and I could see on my walls the shadows of the gulls dropping and rising over the lake. When I told Mrs. Larimer how much I loved the room, she said in a very kind but controlled voice, "That was our Jess's room. She always loved it." After that, I felt the room had been taken away from me.

The Larimers' cabin was the most elegant of all, with a two-storied living room and a massive stone fireplace. I remember how perfect the cabin looked the night I met Bryce. We had been at the Beaches two weeks and Matt was upstairs showering after his sailing lesson. The Larimers were getting ready for the Bradfords, Matt's aunt and uncle, and some other couples to drop by for a drink before dinner. I was sitting in one of the window seats watching Mrs. Larimer trying to find exactly the right arrangement for her heirloom needlepoint-and-velvet cushions. There were Oriental rugs on the polished pine slab floors. Exotic animal heads—trophies from Mr. Larimer's trips to Africa—hung on the walls. The chairs and couches were slipcovered in chintzes that had faded to soft, pale greens and pinks, like a garden looks just minutes before it gets dark.

Mr. Larimer was setting bottles and a silver ice chest out on a wicker teacart. He worked for one of the automobile companies and had something to do with marketing automobiles that took him all over the country. He was a tall man with narrow shoulders and the beginnings of a potbelly. He wore his thinning blond hair a little longer than most of the men at the Beaches, but you didn't have the feeling he was doing it to be trendy but simply because he had other things than a haircut on his mind.

I wasn't surprised that the Larimers were paying no attention to me, but I thought it odd that they paid so little attention to each other. Theirs wasn't the companionable silence of agreement over unspoken things. Instead I had the impression they had found their one subject and just as quickly decided it was something they could not talk about.

Matt came downstairs dragging his feet. "Is it time to eat now?" he asked his grandmother. Because he had spent so little time at the Beaches in the past, it was taking Matt a while to get into the club routine. Matt resented the way his time was organized—tennis and sailing lessons and nature walks and bells to announce meals. He liked nothing better than being by himself, reading a book or just sitting and looking at the lake.

"I haven't heard the bell, Matt," Mrs. Larimer said. "Anyhow, I'd like you and Anne to stay and say hello to Aunt Margot and Uncle Don."

Like Dr. Bradford and Mrs. Larimer, who were brother and sister, half the club seemed to be related to one another. I thought how comforting it would be, in a world where families are scattered and disconnected, to return each summer to a place like the Beaches. I had seen the other members going out of their way to be affectionate and considerate toward the Larimers because of Jess's death. If you were a member of a club like the Beaches, even though something like a divorce happened, you wouldn't be alone. It was like a large extended family—the kind of family people used to have. Although I was a stranger in their Eden, I loved being a part of it.

From the window of the Larimers' cabin I could see the lake stretching to the horizon. In the late afternoon sun it was a sheet of bright moving light. There were a few small fishing boats bobbing on the water, and in the distance you could make out the scrawl of smoke from a freighter. The Bradfords were coming down the boardwalk, Dr. Bradford walking along briskly, his wife trailing behind as though she was not eager to arrive. I saw him look over his shoulder to be sure she was following him. Their faces were glum, as though something unpleasant lay ahead of them, but once they walked through the cabin door they were lively, greeting the Larimers with kisses and hugs.

Dr. Bradford had a boyish face with small features. Everything about him was neat: his small ears, his rather girlish mouth, his tapered fingers with their manicured nails. I knew he was a psychiatrist and I was a little shy meeting him, but to my relief he showed nothing more than a casual interest in me, turning almost immediately to Matt.

"How are you doing, old fellow?" he said. I could see Matt wince at this stilted greeting and wondered that Dr. Bradford didn't notice. "Are you getting some sailing in?"

"Yes, sir. I had a lesson this afternoon."

"It's a thrill, isn't it?"

"Not really." Matt had been in tears that afternoon when the instructor, Bing Roberts, had brought him home. "They made us fall out of the boat on purpose today," Matt told his uncle.

"That was to be sure you could handle an emergency," Mr. Larimer said.

"Why didn't they just ask me? I would have told them I couldn't."

Mrs. Bradford was a small squirrellike woman with bright eyes, a snub nose, short reddish-brown hair, and quick, nervous movements. She had been talking with Mrs. Larimer. Now she turned to Matt. Watching her on the boardwalk, I guessed she was unhappy about something. When she put her arms around Matt, he reacted to her embrace like a startled turtle, drawing himself in. When she let go of him, I could see tears in her eyes. Mrs. Larimer put an arm around her. "Come upstairs, Margot, and see what I've done to the guest suite. I found all of this terrific art deco furniture stashed away in the attic."

When they were out of the room, Mr. Larimer turned to Dr. Bradford. "Margot's still upset," he said.

"We've gone over what happened a thousand times, but she won't be rational about it. I almost decided not to come up this summer, but she has to face it sometime."

They had forgotten Matt and I were in the room. Noticing us, Mr. Larimer said, "Anne, why don't you and Matt wander off toward the lodge? The bell should be sounding any minute for dinner."

Matt didn't like being sent away. "Why have they got all these bells and rules? It's like being in a prison. Why can't we eat right here in our own house like normal people do instead of with a lot of other kids?"

"You're being selfish, Matt," his grandfather said. "This is a vacation for the women, too. They don't want to have to bother with shopping and planning meals."

"Well, somebody has to shop and fix the meals. What about *their* vacation?"

"They're paid to do it, Matt. They have their vacation in the winter when the Beaches is closed."

"Who wants to have a vacation in the winter?"

"That's enough, Matt. You go with Anne."

3

$\mathcal{A}$ boardwalk led to the lodge where the meals were served. Matt disliked having dinner with all the other children and their keepers and was dragging along behind me like a reluctant dog being pulled on an invisible leash. "I hate this place," he said. "I'm supposed to be on a vacation and it's worse than school."

"Lighten up, Matt," I said. "All winter long you kept telling me how eager you were to get up here to the Beaches." Still, it was true that almost every hour of the children's day was regulated. Besides the lessons, there were story hours for the younger children and volleyball competitions for the older ones. With all the regimented activity and with keepers trailing around after them, the children had no time to themselves. The sight of a child just sitting on the beach looking out at the lake was viewed as highly suspicious. Even nature was structured—planned lectures on trees one day, wildflowers or frogs the next.

While I sympathized with Matt, I also envied him, for I was fascinated by the Beaches. At our home money bought necessities with nothing left over for anything else. At the Beaches desire and fulfillment were everywhere. "Stop feeling sorry for yourself," I told him. "This is a terrific place to spend your summer."

"I'd rather be back in Lakeville."

"What did you do there in the summertime?"

"I didn't do anything—that was the good part. Dad worked as a fishing guide and Mom was always busy fixing up the house, so they just pushed me out the door. I had this neat shack I built from driftwood I found on the beach near where we lived. Sometimes Mom would make me sandwiches to eat and I could be gone all day. You can find great stuff on the beach: gull feathers and fossils and colored glass that's worn all smooth and shells and net floats. Once when I was in Lakeville I found a sandpiper with a broken wing and I took care of it in my shack until it got well."

"Didn't you and your parents do things together?" I was thinking of all the picnics and trips to beaches and parks and zoos I had gone on with my own parents, memories that had become bittersweet.

"My parents didn't like to be together."

"That's an odd thing to say, Matt."

"What did you ask me for if you didn't want me to tell you the truth? You're like my grandparents. Just because my mom died you want me to pretend everything used to be terrific. And I'm not even supposed to mention my dad. Like, when I say his name everyone gets this look on their faces as if there was a bad smell in the room, and they won't let me see him and they won't tell me why I can't."

It was the first time Matt had mentioned his father to me. His voice was choked and shrill, as though he was trying not to cry. I didn't look at him. The bell for the children's dinner hadn't rung yet, so we stopped to sit on one of the benches on the boardwalk. Like everything else at the Beaches, the bench was old but in perfect condition, the black wrought iron newly painted and the teak carefully oiled. At the Beaches things seemed to go on forever. Even the pots of begonias with their bright yellow and red blossoms on the cabin porches never seemed to wilt or die. I knew the Larimers must still be unhappy over their daughter's death: I could see how much they were grieving, but I was stupid enough then to think there was a kind of comfort or dignity, even beauty, to suffering when it was done in a setting like the Beaches.

The children's dinner hour was my least favorite time of day. With no adults at the tables except the keepers, all of whom, like me, were in their late teens, the children reverted to primitive manners, grabbing and throwing food, talking with disgustingly full mouths, spilling milk, and shouting complaints or compliments at the kitchen. When the adults had their dinner the tables were set with linen cloths and a waitress served the food. At the children's meals, after interminable arguments about whose turn it was, someone from each table brought the plates from the kitchen and at the end of the meal cleared away the dishes. I guessed that somewhere along the line the club members had decided it would be instructive for the children to have some sort of "task" or "responsibility."

Besides the tables of children with their keepers, there was a table of older children who were careful to keep their distance from their younger brothers and sisters, as if being little were catching. They spoke in whispers and if you came within listening distance of their table there was total silence. They did everything they could to set themselves apart, including sneaking cigarettes and substituting wine coolers for their fruit juice.

The cook, Mabel, was the wife of Lyle Neeb, the security man at the Beaches. The Neebs lived in Lakeville. I wondered if they were the ones that Mrs. Larimer thought might gossip to me about what had happened to Jess. Sleeping in Jess's room had made me even more curious about her. But apart from commenting about Matt— "He's too quiet for his own good"— all Mabel ever said was, "I never understood why a nice girl like Jess Larimer would live in a dump like Lakeville. It doesn't even have a traffic light."

"But you live there," I said.

"With me it's not optional."

"How did Jess meet Bryce Stevens?" I asked.

"When Bryce's dad, Len, worked here, Bryce used to come and help him. He'd guide the members when they went trout fishing on the Sandy River. He doesn't know it as well as Thomas does, though."

Thomas was an Ottawa Indian who had been around the Beaches for as long as anyone could remember. He worked as a maintenance man. "Does Thomas guide?"

"Not Thomas," Mabel said. "He figures this property used to belong to his ancestors and he's not going to let anything else on the property get away from him, even the fish."

At our table in the dining room there were two giggling girls a year or two older than Matt: Susan Stockton and Meredith Thompson. They both had a crush on Ed Lindner. He was attractive, tall and lean. With his slicked-back hair and classic profile, he would have been perfect in one of those ads for retro clothes—white linen suits or belted suit jackets with knickers. Ed was a keeper and the "naturalist" for the Beaches. He conducted walks along the beach and in the woods for the children. That evening the girls had drawn a big heart with their initials and Ed's on it and had placed the picture under Ed's plate. They were crazy with suspense waiting for him to finish his meal so the plate could be removed and he would see the picture.

Most of the keepers were the older brothers or sisters

or cousins of their charges, bribed into taking a job they obviously loathed. Ed and I were the exceptions. Syrie Stockton was a keeper for her sister Susan in exchange for having been allowed to go to Bennington instead of Vassar. For watching over her sister Meredith, Terry Thompson was getting a car. I liked Terry and Syrie, but after two minutes we ran out of things to talk about.

I knew they considered me too serious, a trait that had a low value at the Beaches. I had to admit they were right. I've never been able to make small talk. And besides my inability to make small talk, I was an outsider.

I was pleased that Ed Lindner was also an outsider. Ed came from Lakeville, where his father owned a hardware store. He went to the local community college in Sand Point. I suppose he had been made the resident naturalist on the theory that he came from the area and should know what there was to see. I felt sorry for Ed because Robin Beamish, the boy he looked after, was impossible. He was a whiner who nagged people into playing checkers or cards and then cheated. One by one, he had lost his friends. At first, when Matt didn't know anyone at the Beaches, he had made friends with Robin, but Matt had quickly become impatient with Robin's antics and began to go out of his way to avoid him. He felt sorry for Robin, though, and I had never heard Matt call Robin the Grub (Robin resisted the outdoors, and his plump body was a kind of translucent white) like all the other children did. Knowing that Matt was one of the few children left who would tolerate him, Robin usually headed for our table.

That evening Robin was telling in excruciating detail the plot of one of an endless series of science-fiction stories he had made up to get attention. "So these giant grasshoppers eat up everything they see that's green— money and green cars and people wearing green clothes." Robin illustrated the story by chomping away at his salad with large, noisy bites. Shreds of lettuce dribbled out of his mouth. Matt, half revolted and half hypnotized, was watching the performance.

"Robin," Syrie said, "you've got the table manners of a cow. Shape up or I'm going to tell your mother what a pig you are."

"Make up your mind," Robin said, salad falling out of his mouth. "Which am I, a cow or a pig? Anyhow, it takes one to know one." He was pleased with his retort.

Ed groaned. "Shut up, Robin." He turned to me. "Want to drive over to Lakeville after Matt and Robin are tucked into bed? I'll treat you to something from the Dairy Queen with my hard-earned money. I've got to get away from this place for a couple of hours or I'm going to turn into cardboard like everyone else here, present company excepted." Ed made a show of pretending to dislike the Beaches, but like me, he was a little dazzled. He was pleased that in spite of being a local he had been chosen to spend the summer at the Beaches. He had a kind of self-conscious shyness that made him a favorite with the little girls like Susan and Meredith, who followed him around and were pathetically grateful when he took any notice of them.

I watched him pick up his empty plate. When he saw the picture the girls had drawn, he blushed. In his hurry to crumple it, he knocked over his water glass, sending the girls into fits of giggles. I helped mop up the mess and, feeling sorry for him, promised to drive into Lakeville later that evening. "I'll see you around nine," I told him. Susan and Meredith gave me envious looks. The truth was, I wasn't that eager to spend the evening at the Larimers' cabin. They were very nice to me, but they seemed preoccupied. When you talked to them it was like they were swimming up from some deep ocean to answer you, and when the conversation was over, back down they went.

Ed was getting up a volleyball game. Robin was trying to get out of playing. "I'm always getting hit by the ball," he whined.

"You're going to play," Ed told him, "to make up for that second dessert you scarfed down. And if you tell me you don't want to, we'll use you for the ball. You're getting round enough."

Syrie said, "Come on, Annie, you and Matt can be on our team." Like most of the members of the Beaches, she tended to be solicitous of Matt.

I looked at Matt. "I don't feel like it," he said.

"Guess we'll go for a walk," I said. "See you later." I was eager to get away from all the squirming bodies and

22

tennis shoe smells of the dining room, and I was feeling a little homesick. I longed to be someplace I belonged. I had been at the Beaches for two weeks, and apart from no longer getting lost on the paths through the woods and being able to identify who lived in which cabin, I was still a stranger. References were constantly being made to things that had happened in past years. For dessert that night we had been served strawberry pie, which set off an argument between Syrie and Terry as to which cook over the years had made the best pastry. Even Robin had been able to contribute to the discussion, which had gone on and on. It was like that with everything—reminiscences about the year the barge with the Fourth of July fireworks had exploded on the lake, the year the tennis pro had sprained his ankle at the beginning of the season, the year the alewives had washed up on shore and there had been no swimming, the year some of the club members had surprised the Clementses, who had a habit of going skinny-dipping late at night, by hiding their towels. It wasn't that Ed and I were purposely left out—everyone was careful to explain to us what they were talking about—but it was no fun living in a world that always had to be explained to you. And then I felt sorry for Matt. Although the Beaches was as alien to him as it was to me, he was supposed to belong.

4

Matt and I stood outside the dining room waiting for one of us to decide what direction to take. "How come you get to go to Lakeville with Ed and I never get to go back there? I haven't even seen the kids I went to school with."

"Why don't you ask your grandparents if you can go?"

"I did. They said it was more important for me to get used to the Beaches and make friends here."

"Why didn't you spend more time at the Beaches when you were growing up in Lakeville?" I asked him. Matt started off along the path to Grass Lake and I trailed along.

"I used to come to the Beaches with my dad in the

fall when everyone at the club was gone. Dad didn't get along too well with the club members. We'd shoot wild turkeys and grouse."

"Didn't Lyle have something to say about that?"

"They didn't have a security guard then. Just Thomas."

"What did Thomas say?"

"I think he did a little shooting himself. Anyhow, Thomas never says anything."

It was true. If you met Thomas on one of the paths and said hello, he would just look at you. It wasn't an unfriendly look, only a suggestion that all loose talk was a waste of time. He was some unfathomable age, his face accordioned into creases. He paid no attention to me, but he was fond of Matt and often had something in his pocket to give him—a stone of fossilized coral from the beach or a feather from some colorful bird like a jay or a goldfinch. Once he gave Matt a bundle of sweet grass that Matt kept in a box. Each time you opened the box there was a wonderful fresh odor that smelled like the beginning of the world. Thomas carried on his work or left it just as he pleased, seemingly indifferent to what the members of the club thought of him. I had seen him turn and walk away while Dr. Bradford was still talking to him.

Grass Lake was the most remote of the lakes owned by the Beaches. It was on the eastern border of the club property, a walk of about a mile from the lodge. Few people went there. Mallard Lake had better fishing and Birch Lake better swimming. Grass Lake was shallow with a soft marl bottom. It was fringed around with dark green hemlock trees whose reflection gave the water a shadowed, murky look. The herons, who had a rookery there, were the lake's attraction. They circled the lake, their long necks folded into an S-shape, their feet dragging awkwardly in the air. Or you saw them wading with a slow, high goose step, their long bills ready to spear frogs half submerged in the mud along the shore.

On our way to the lake I kept questioning Matt, still puzzled at why he had spent so little time at the Beaches. "Didn't you even see your grandparents?"

"Mom used to come to see them, but it made Dad angry if she took me. He said the Beaches would turn me into a terminal preppy. I think he was hurt about what happened to his dad. Grandpa Stevens died and Dad blamed the Beaches."

"Why did he blame the Beaches?"

"Dad said Grandpa died of a broken heart."

We had reached Grass Lake and Matt, tired of answering my questions, ran on ahead of me. Suddenly he stopped. A man was standing on the shore watching us. The lowering sun was in my eyes and I wasn't sure who it was—Lyle making his rounds or some member of the club, although that was unlikely because it was the adults' dinnertime. I saw Matt start toward the man, slowly at first and then more quickly, looking over his shoulder at me as though I might stop him.

Watching Matt, I guessed who it was and panicked, remembering how upset Mrs. Larimer had been when she mentioned Bryce's name, and how she had warned me against letting Matt see his father. What would the Larimers say when they found out Matt had been with Bryce? I thought of shouting to Matt to come back, but that seemed overly dramatic. I didn't know what else I could do. Bryce and Matt stood together at the lake's edge, watching me come toward them. It was only a few hundred feet, but it seemed to take me forever. Because they were watching me, all of my movements seemed clumsy. When I finally reached them Matt said, "Her name is Annie. She's my keeper."

Bryce was smiling a wide, disarming smile. He was blond, his hair and beard bleached by the sun and almost white against his dark tan. His eyes were that bright blue that seems startling in a man. He wore faded jeans and a white shirt that had been washed to a soft thinness. The sleeves were rolled up, exposing tan, muscular arms. There was a sense, so strong it was almost a presence, of physical magnetism. I understood why Jess was willing to stay on in Lakeville. There was also something about Bryce that suggested he knew just how attractive he was.

"You look like you've seen the devil," he said. "So I suppose you've guessed who I am. What have they been telling you about me?"

I was ashamed of the alarm he must have seen on my face. He seemed so friendly and Matt was obviously glad to see him. I began to relax a little. He held out his hand. I took it, trying to smile. Since then I have often thought that one gesture, the putting of my hand into his, was the beginning of all our trouble. It led to deceit and betrayal and worse. It changed our lives forever.

Matt was watching us. "I don't care what my grandparents say. Why can't I see you?" he asked Bryce. "This club is a prison. They make you do something every minute. I've got tennis lessons and sailing lessons and even at night they've got all these activities in case someone just tries to sit still for ten minutes, and when I'm not doing all that stuff I can't be alone anyhow because Annie is always trailing around after me."

"She's just doing her job, Matt," Bryce said. "It's not her fault."

I was grateful to him for taking my side.

"So why can't I see you?"

"Because Annie would tell your grandparents and then they really wouldn't let you out of their sight."

"Are you going to tell about tonight, Annie?" Matt was looking at me, his face working as though he was trying to hold back tears.

I was uneasy at being there with Bryce. I remembered the look on Mrs. Larimer's face when she was impressing me with the need to keep Matt away from Bryce. She would be furious if she found out about the meeting and might even send me back home. But what could I do to stop the meeting? Certainly I couldn't forcibly drag Matt away. Matt's question suggested an answer. "I won't tell your grandparents if you promise to come home with me right now."

Ignoring me, Matt asked Bryce, "Why don't you take me back to Lakeville with you?"

"For one thing, your friend Annie here would have the whole club after me, to say nothing of the sheriff. We wouldn't get two miles from here. Anyhow, I don't have any place to take you. I'm not staying in Lakeville. I'm holing up in an old cabin outside of town. I'll tell you what. If I promise Annie not to try to see you again, maybe she'll take a message from me to you every once in a while and let me know how you are." He turned to me. "There can't be any harm in just sending a word to my own son. I mean, it's bad enough that I can't ever see him. The Beaches has a lot of influence and they got a judge to go along with them. Don't think they didn't promise him a payoff of some kind so they could get sole custody of Matt."

I half believed him. I was so impressed with the wealth and position of the club members that I thought they might be able to do almost anything. When I saw how happy Matt was to see his father I thought the Larimers selfish. What about Bryce's grief over losing Jess? I sympathized with Bryce; like me, he didn't belong to the Beaches. And there was something else. I was thinking how much I missed my own father, how hard it was to have him so far away and never to see him. "I'll think about it," I said.

"My cabin's not too far from here, so I can drop by anytime," Bryce said.

"What about the security man, Lyle?"

"I could stand two feet from him and he wouldn't know I was there," Bryce said. "Apart from Thomas the only one who knew this place as well as I do was my dad, and he's dead. I used to spend all summer here trailing around after him. I can show you things here you'd never find on your own, things no one at the Beaches knows about. The Beaches just *think* they know this place. Matt's great-great-grandfather cleared the timber on ten thousand acres around the Beaches and kept a whole mile along Lake Michigan for himself so he could start up this club, but all he cared about was using the land—timbering it, hunting and fishing on it, and then building these mansions. He might have spent some time here, but he never really *saw* what was around him."

Bryce smiled at me. "I'll show you what I mean. Look at this tree. See the holes that look almost square? They were made by a pileated woodpecker. I'll leave notes here for you to give Matt, and you can leave a note or two for me. Just let me know how Matt is. That's all I ask. If you say yes, I'll be on my way."

Matt was looking at me. I nodded, eager to agree to anything that would allow me to get Matt away from Bryce. Later, once Matt was safely back at the cabin, I could change my mind if I wanted to. I could forget all about Bryce. Matt looked surprised when I nodded my approval. Afterward I wondered if he expected me to say no. Maybe he wanted me to, without quite knowing it himself. Matt was too honest, really, to want to sneak around behind anyone's back. For a moment I had the uncomfortable feeling that Matt was disappointed in me for giving in to Bryce. Then Matt said, "You're almost human, Annie," and grinned.

Something occurred to me. "How did you know we would be coming to Grass Lake?" I asked. "We didn't know ourselves."

"I've been watching you for days," Bryce said, and grinned.

I wasn't sure I liked the idea of being watched; it was an eerie sensation, and I began to think I ought to tell the Larimers after all. Bryce must have seen my doubt because suddenly he asked, "How are you getting on at the Beaches?"

"It's an incredible place and everyone is so nice to me, but it's like a secret society," I said. I felt Bryce of all people would understand that. "It doesn't seem to matter how long I'm here. As soon as I learn one thing, I find something else I don't understand."

"Yes," he said, "I've been through that. It won't get any better. What hurts is that Matt will have to live with them and either be an outsider or what's worse, gradually become one of them. Then I'd lose him like I lost Jess. I won't let that happen." For the first time the smile and easy manner were gone and I saw someone else, someone both hurt and angry.

He must have been embarrassed to have let me see his real feelings because he quickly said, "Let me show you and Matt something else." He led us to a grassy spot along the lake's edge. "There," he said.

"I don't see anything," Matt said.

"There," Bryce said again, and pointed. And suddenly we could see it. In a slight indentation in the ground, lined with grasses and leaves, were three creamy eggs speckled with lavender.

Matt was excited. "What is it?" His voice was hushed, as it always was when he was looking at something alive—a mouse or even a grasshopper or a cricket.

"Least sandpiper's nest," Bryce said.

"We can check it each day," I told Matt, "and see when they hatch."

"No," Bryce said. "Stay away from the nest or you'll leave a scent trail for some raccoon or fox to follow."

How dangerous everything was, I thought. I forgot about wanting to tell the Larimers. I was sure you could trust someone who could discover the hidden nests of sandpipers. And showing us the nest, Bryce's voice was tender.

Bryce ran his hand through Matt's hair. "I'm taking off, Matt. I don't want to get your friend here in trouble. I really appreciate this," he said to me. "Whenever you have the chance, leave a note in the tree letting me know how Matt is, and I'll leave some word for Matt." He put a hand on my shoulder and looked at me as though everything depended on me. It was a heady feeling.

I decided the Larimers were snobbish and didn't want Bryce around Matt because Bryce came from Lakeville and didn't fit into the Beaches. I felt sorry for Matt. He had suddenly been thrown in with the other children at the Beaches, with whom he had nothing in common. Like me, he felt an outsider. I had seen the way the other children would go off, assuming Matt would trail along, and Matt, feeling too shy to follow them, would wait for some kind of invitation, some special effort on their part. They would finally make the effort, but you could see they thought it a nuisance.

Matt and I watched Bryce turn onto a path that led away from the club. Bryce had picked up a stick and was hitting it absent-mindedly against the tree trunks as he walked along. We heard the sharp thwack repeated long after we lost sight of him in the darkness that was filling the spaces between the trees.

Matt and I stood looking out over the small lake, both of us thinking about Bryce and neither of us saying anything. On the opposite shore a hawk was gliding in wide circles. "He's after something," Matt said. We couldn't see his prey. It might have been a chipmunk or a vole, some small animal, foolish or injured in some way.

"I'm going over and scare the hawk off," Matt said. He took care of birds with injured wings, crippled mice, grounded butterflies whose fine dusty scales had been rubbed from their wings. His worry even spread to up-rooted plants. He protected life at all levels, as though everything could be patched up, made whole again, even when his own life suggested the opposite.

I watched him run along the shore. He disappeared for several seconds among the thick branches of the hemlocks that arched over the shore and I started after him, but then he came into view again. I guessed he had only stopped to examine a pretty stone or some animal lair at the base of a tree—a fox's or a mink's. He had nearly reached the spot the hawk was circling when the large bird made a sudden downward swoop. A moment later the hawk was soaring over the trees. I was too far away to see if it had its prey, but when Matt returned I could tell from the way his feet dragged he had been too late, or worse, his approach had flushed the small animal from its cover out into the open where the hawk was waiting.

Walking back, Matt said with a sudden burst of feeling, "Thanks for letting me talk to my dad. Just knowing he's around will make a lot of difference. I'll feel more like I belong here. He and my mom used to argue a lot, but he was always nice to me." I was thinking about Bryce too. Away from him I was less sure of his easy friendliness. In retrospect it seemed too practiced, like the smoothness of someone with a plan. Still, I believed the summer would be more exciting now; if the Beaches had their secrets, I would have mine, too.

5

When we returned to the Larimers' cabin that evening I was afraid Matt would give our meeting with Bryce away, but he was all innocence. I decided he was used to keeping secrets and wondered what the secrets were and from whom he hid them. Mrs. Larimer made a point of spending some time with Matt before he went to bed. "You have a long-enough day, Anne," she said, but I suspected she welcomed the time with her grandson.

I went outside, relieved to be leaving the Larimers' cabin but sorry I had promised to drive to Lakeville with Ed. I wanted to be by myself so I could sort out my feelings about Bryce. Until that evening I had seen him through the Larimers' eyes—someone who might do Matt harm. Having met him, I didn't believe it was possible. I tried to think what Jess would have wanted for Matt. Even if Jess and Bryce's marriage was in trouble, it was hard to believe Jess wouldn't want Matt to see his father. I couldn't understand why Jess had stopped caring for Bryce; he didn't seem like someone it would be easy to stop loving. At least, I thought, the evening wouldn't be entirely wasted. I could get Ed to tell me what he knew about Bryce.

Ed was waiting in his car for me at the club entrance. Before I could ask about Bryce, I had to listen to Ed's complaints about Robin. "He's the worst. There isn't enough money in the world to pay me for putting up with him. I tried to talk to his dad tonight, man-to-man stuff. You know, 'Sir, I just thought you might want to know that that son of yours is a real pain in the ass.' What I really said in my best social-worker style was, 'I wonder if we could dialogue a little about Robin, who seems to be disgustingly Oedipal, or to put it another way, a spoiled mother's boy.' To tell you the truth, Robin's parents don't want to hear anything about him. It's like it was bad enough giving birth to a monster like that, and now they're glad he's someone else's problem."

"The Larimers are too much the other way," I said. "They never give Matt a minute alone. I don't know what they're afraid of." We were driving through Eagletown. Eagletown lies between the Beaches and

Lakeville. It's an Indian town with a few small white clapboard houses and two or three trailers. "Does Thomas live here?" I asked Ed.

"Thomas and all of his relatives."

"What exactly does Thomas do?"

"He fixes anything that needs fixing, but what he really does is keep an eye on everyone. Thomas has worked for the Beaches for years. If he wanted to talk, which he certainly doesn't, he could tell plenty."

"What's there to tell? I can't believe any of the people at the Beaches would do something scandalous."

"That's because you're a romantic. If you had lived in Lakeville all your life like I have, you'd have a different view of the Beaches."

We were coming into Lakeville. The main street was lined with white frame houses, run-down and dilapidated. The only one in good repair was a funeral home. Beyond the houses you could see empty fields and scrubby woods. Also on the main street was the hardware store owned by Ed's dad, a new supermarket, a five-and-dime with cheap swimsuits and garish beach towels in the window, and a drugstore advertising a two-for-one sale on vitamins. At one end of the main street there was a township hall with a library in the basement. At the other end was a bar with a flashing neon sign advertising country music on Saturday night. Across the street from the bar was the Dairy Queen. I thought it no wonder people gossiped about the Beaches. There was nothing else to do.

"What will it be, Dairy Queen or the bar?" Ed asked.

"The Larimers would never approve of me coming back to the Beaches smelling of beer."

"You're too anxious to please those people. They're no better than anyone else."

We sat in Ed's car drinking strawberry milk shakes. In the next car four teenagers were watching us. The girls, fifteen or sixteen, heavily made up and wearing T-shirts, were flirting with Ed. I tried to imagine how Jess Larimer managed to live in Lakeville with Bryce. "I don't want to hurt your feelings," I said, "but what is there to do here in the winter?" I imagined the cold wind blowing off the lake and down Lakeville's empty streets, the plastic wreaths that would stay on the lamp-posts for months after Christmas, and the high school kids out in front of the cut-rate drugstore every night, just standing there shivering. "I mean, what did Jess and Bryce do?"

"You mean, what did someone as classy as Jess do in a boring, end-of-the-universe town like Lakeville where only a hick like me could survive?"

He was smiling, so I said, "Yes, I guess that's just what I mean."

"You city people are so naive. You don't know about Friday night high school basketball or Sunday afternoon potluck church suppers."

"Did Jess really go to things like that?"

"She was a damn good sport, at the beginning, any-how. Of course I wasn't even in high school when they first came to Lakeville, but my older sister worked at the library, where they file all the rumors. Jess got up a wardrobe from L. L. Bean—lots of corduroy slacks and flannel shirts. I think she even went to some of the Amway parties and bought soap powder and window cleaner with the rest of the town's high society. When Matt started school, Jess used to volunteer at the library. That's when my sister really got to know her. By then Jess had had it, though she didn't do much complaining out loud."

"You mean she was sick of the town?"

"I think she could have stuck out the town if it weren't for Bryce."

"Well, then, why did she marry him?" By now we had finished our milk shakes and were the only car left in the parking lot. Ed had an arm around me and I could see he was ready to make some moves. I wanted to get out of there, but I didn't want to stop talking about Jess and Bryce, especially Bryce.

"She was going through a back-to-nature period when she met him. You know, getting up at six in the morning and tramping through the woods with binoculars, spying on the birdies. It was a kind of reaction formation to the Beaches and that preppy suburb you both come from."

"My mom and I don't live the way the Larimers do," I protested.

"You don't live like we do, either," Ed said. "When you were a kid you were probably getting all dressed up on Saturday morning and going down to the art museum with your folks to look at five-hundred-year-old pictures, while I was bagging groceries."

I had to laugh because it was exactly what my family used to do. My folks never missed an opportunity to rub my nose in art or music. "What attracted her to Bryce?" I persisted.

"The question isn't what she saw in Bryce but what he saw in her. All the girls in Lakeville ran after Bryce. And Jess was no Miss America. She had a big backside and big feet and wore serious glasses. I always thought Bryce just wanted to take something away from the Beaches, but I'm not the most objective person. I never particularly liked him.

"Bryce used to work with his dad, who was the caretaker at the Beaches. Bryce always knew where all the flora and fauna were. I suppose Jess thought it would be like living at Walden Pond to live here in Lakeville with him. We heard from the Neebs that after Bryce and Jess got married, Bryce had to quit his job at the Beaches because the club thought it was a little awkward to have the husband of a member's daughter sawing their wood and shoveling their snow. So Bryce worked as an electrician in the winter and guided fisherman in the summer. Rumor had it that Mr. Larimer gave Jess some money for their wedding and she and Bryce bought an old farmhouse outside of town. Fixing it up kept her busy. I know she was getting money on the side from her family because my sister said she saw a lot of things in the house that Bryce could never have afforded. She said they looked like Jess must have bought them in Blue Harbor."

Blue Harbor was an upscale resort town about twenty miles on the other side of Lakeville. "But Matt says they never spent any time at the Beaches," I said. "I don't understand that. Lakeville is so close by."

"Unfortunately, the year after Bryce and Jess got married, members at the club discovered that Len Stevens, Bryce's dad, had some sort of poaching ring going. He was shooting game on the Beaches' property and selling it."

"Did Bryce have anything to do with it?"

"No. It was strictly his old man. At least that's what they said at the Beaches. Bryce's dad denied the whole thing and blamed it on Thomas. Bryce was sure his father was innocent, and when the Beaches kicked his dad out, Bryce never forgave the club. He wouldn't let Jess or Matt visit. I think she sneaked over there from time to time, but she was afraid to take Matt because he would have told Bryce."

I was tugging at Ed's arm, trying to get it back on the steering wheel. "Time to go home," I said.

Ed leaned over and kissed me. "That's my reward for giving you all the gossip on the Beaches. Next time we're going to talk about *you*. I like you, Annie. I just hope you don't get too involved with the Beaches. You're a real person and that's not a real world."

When we got back to the Beaches, Ed left for the

Beamish cabin and I headed along the boardwalk for the Larimers'. It was a moonless night and I made my way from long stretches of darkness to the patches of light the cabin windows made. Just before I reached the Larimers' cabin, I left the boardwalk and walked down to the edge of the beach. During my first few weeks at the Beaches, I had been drawn to Ed and thought something might come of our summer together. I knew he liked me, but for me some chemistry was lacking between us. I would have been happy if we could just have stayed friends. I wanted someone to talk to about my feelings about the Beaches. But I knew Ed wouldn't settle for that. The trouble was, although I tried not to think of Bryce as anything other than Matt's father, I knew I was attracted to him in a way I wasn't attracted to Ed.

In the few hours I had been away from the lake I had forgotten the persistent sound of the waves washing onto the shore. I edged toward the water and, misjudging the waves, felt water splash over my shoes. As I jumped backward I saw a figure on the beach moving toward me. For a moment I thought it might be Bryce, but it was only Thomas. "Hello," I said, trying not to sound startled. He walked right by me without a word. A porch light went on and for a moment I had a glimpse of his face. His expression was not unfriendly, but watchful, as though I were embarked on some risky journey too foolish to speak of.

6

In the next few days Matt kept asking me if I had heard from his father. Although I thought of Bryce all the time, I was too nervous and guilty about my meeting with him to look for messages at Grass Lake. Mrs. Larimer must have noticed my preoccupation, because on the third day after my meeting with Bryce she took me aside. "Anne," she said in that pleasant, even voice that was at once friendly and controlled, "why don't you take tomorrow off and have some fun? No one can spend all week with a ten-year-old and not feel a little bored. Mr. Larimer and some of the other members are going out on our boat for the day to do a little fishing and Matt can go with them. Why don't you take our

43

station wagon and drive into Blue Harbor? I have a couple of errands for you and the rest of the day is yours.

"I hope the summer is working out for you, Anne. For our part, we're more than happy with you."

I was pleased to hear her praise, but I couldn't help wondering what Mrs. Larimer would say if she knew about my meeting with Bryce. I mumbled something about no boy wanting a girl trailing after him all the time.

"Matt likes you very much. He's said that to us. Of course he'd rather be on his own, but he knows the club rules. I'm only sorry he isn't working harder at making friends with the other children. Mr. Larimer and I feel at a disadvantage because we're so much older. That's why it will be good for Matt to go on the fishing trip. Some of the other boys like Robin Beamish and Lance Brightman will be along with their dads."

That they hadn't noticed how Matt disliked Robin proved how out of touch the Larimers were. I was happy, though, to have a day off to look forward to. For the first time, I was eager to get away from the Beaches.

The Larimers' cruiser was docked at the marina in Blue Harbor. Although Matt had seen the boat ("Six people can sleep on it, Annie, and it has a TV and two bathrooms they call 'heads.' "), this was his first chance to go out on it. He was almost enthusiastic, but he didn't want me to notice. "I suppose Robin is going to fall into the lake and ruin the fishing," he said. "I don't know why they have to take him. I'm a lot better at fishing than he is."

"Where did you learn to fish?"

"My dad used to take me fishing out on Lake Michigan. You should have seen the size of the salmon and lake trout he caught. If he could go out with us tomorrow, he'd really show everyone how to fish."

When I thought how happy Matt would have been to have his father on the boat with him, keeping Bryce and Matt apart seemed heartless, and I felt less guilty about Matt's meeting with Bryce.

On the way to Blue Harbor the next morning I passed through Lakeville with little more than a glance, but once on the other side of town I drove more slowly. I knew from questioning Matt that the farmhouse he had lived in with Jess and Bryce was on the road I was traveling, but one farmhouse looked like another to me. Some were unpainted with old cars rusting in the backyard and angry dogs chained to a tree. A few had been carefully restored. Those homes had grapevine wreaths on their front doors, baskets of hanging flowers, and neat vegetable gardens. You could imagine what the insides looked like—the refinished woodwork, the old pine furniture, and the quilts on the fourposter beds. One of those houses had probably been Bryce and Jess's. I thought it odd that Bryce was no longer living in their home but was "holing up in an old cabin." Probably he didn't want the Larimers to know he was back. But why? Then I was approaching the outskirts of Blue Harbor and decided I would put those questions out of my mind and enjoy my day off.

When she handed me her list of errands, Mrs. Larimer

had given me a fifty-dollar bill. "That's for you, Anne," she said. At first I tried to return it. I knew she meant well, but I was embarrassed to have money given to me in that way—like a tip—but she insisted. "I know what it was like for Jess to go into Blue Harbor after she was married and see all those pretty things and not be able to afford them. I have to admit we helped her out every once in a while, although I'm not sure that was wise. But there's no reason I can't spoil you a little. We're so pleased with you. Buy something for yourself and don't spend it too carefully. Give yourself a treat."

It was what I planned to do. My job as keeper paid well, and with no expenses I had put nearly all of my salary aside for college that fall. I felt as though I deserved a treat—and the town was full of temptations. Many of the shops divided their year between Blue Harbor in the summer and the expensive towns of Florida in the winter. You could find hand-knitted sweaters, alligator moccasins, old painted furniture from Sweden. I wandered through the shops in a daze of longing, too intimidated to even ask for help.

The streets were crowded with tanned, smartly dressed people, some of them on expensive errands, some of them simply wandering from store to store, knowing something would catch their eye. I tried to imagine Bryce in Blue Harbor, sure he would never come to such a place. I wondered if it was fair for the Larimers to have given money to their daughter so that she could come here without Bryce knowing about it. It seemed sneaky.

After a day of shopping at Blue Harbor it would have been hard for Jess to go back to their house in Lakeville; it would seem so much less than it was when she left it. And Bryce would sense that.

Mrs. Larimer's gift to me of the fifty dollars was no longer the windfall it had been in the morning. It would buy very little in Blue Harbor stores. I decided to save the money for a place where it would have some value. Across the street I saw Syrie and Terry with some other girls from the Beaches. They were piling into Syrie's new car, their arms full of packages. Syrie saw me and came over. She was wearing a scarlet shirt with khaki shorts and some expensive Italian sandals I had admired in one of the shops, sandals that would have cost me a week's salary. "Why didn't you tell us you were coming?" she asked. "We could have all driven in together."

I mumbled something about having errands to do for Mrs. Larimer.

"Poor woman, she keeps buying and buying and it doesn't do any good. She'll never get over Jess's death. God, what a relief to get away from the brats. They're all out fishing and I hope they fall overboard." Actually she and her sister Susan got along very well. Susan adored Syrie. "Listen, don't miss that new European shop. They have these marvelous silk ski jackets from Austria. And if you're thinking of coming to Mother's talk tonight, don't. I repeat, don't."

Mrs. Stockton was giving a lecture on recycling in

the lodge that evening. From time to time club members gave informal presentations on their favorite subject—Syrie's father had given a demonstration on tying flies, Dr. Bradford was going to talk to the children about the stars. "What Mother is going to do is have a BYOB party. Everyone is supposed to bring their own garbage bag and then she's going to make them take out everything and tell them how it can be recycled. How would you like to have a mother who was *earnest*? See you back at the jail." She was gone.

My afternoon at Blue Harbor made me feel more than ever an outsider at the Beaches. Families who buy together stay together, I thought. I was feeling sorry for Bryce, and after dropping off Mrs. Larimer's things I headed for Grass Lake. I think I had some idea of acting as peacemaker, finding a way to bring Bryce and the Larimers together. I even imagined a scene of tender reconciliation with myself as the heroine. Almost against my will I looked in the tree where Bryce said he would leave a message and found a note with no signature and no date: MEET ME HERE IN THE MORNING WHILE MATT IS HAVING HIS SAILING LESSON. The note could have been there for several days. Bryce, I thought guiltily, would have come to the lake each day looking for me. I knew I would be there the next morning, all the while promising myself it would be the last time.

That evening Matt and I were sitting on the cabin steps watching the club members walking toward the lodge, dutifully lugging their trash bags to Mrs. Stockton's lecture. Matt asked me, as he did every evening, "Have you heard anything from my father?"

"I found a note. I'll meet him tomorrow morning."

"Let me go with you," he pleaded.

"That wasn't the agreement. Besides, you have your sailing lesson. Look, I shouldn't be doing this at all." Matt must have been afraid that I would change my mind about meeting Bryce, because he gave up coaxing. I didn't like that kind of power. I didn't want to be the one to decide whether or not Matt should see his father.

7

*B*ryce's first words to me the next morning were, "I've missed you." I was pleased. I wanted to be more than just a messenger. I told Bryce about my trip to Blue Harbor. "Those people think they can buy up the world," he said. "Come on, I'll show you what they've got right here they don't even know about, and it's worth a lot more than anything they could find in that town."

"Matt is great," I said, eager to assure myself that I was seeing Bryce out of concern for Matt and not for any reasons of my own. "He went fishing yesterday on his grandfather's boat."

"I know all about that," Bryce said. "And they weren't fishing. I don't call it fishing when you have someone take you to a spot, hand you a pole with the bait al-

ready on it, and point down into the lake and say 'there.'
Matt and I did some real fishing, but he's probably forgotten everything I taught him. Just once before the
summer is over I'd like to go fishing with him again."

We were scrambling down a bank through bracken
tall enough to brush my face. "Look at that," Bryce
said. Below us was a dense mat of moss, a giant green
raft suspended in a pool of black water.

"What is it?" I asked.

"It's a bog. One of the last ones left in this part of
the state. Developers like Earl Beamish have filled in
the rest of them. It's sphagnum moss held together with
the roots from azalea and leatherleaf."

He led me onto the raft, which trembled and swayed
under my feet. "Be careful," he warned me. "There are
holes in the moss where you could go under. Once you
disturb the sphagnum it takes years for it to grow back."
He was proud and possessive, as if he truly owned what
he was showing me. He was no longer someone who
had stolen onto another man's property. He was the
king in disguise, wandering unrecognized through his
kingdom.

He pointed out sundews with faces like tiny suns, their
rays hung with globes of dew. He showed me pitcher
plants, cranberries, and heathers. We were halfway
around the circle of the bog when Bryce stopped abruptly.
"Orchids," he said. "This species is rare. I've never seen
them anywhere else." They were like small lavender birds,
their tiny fringed wings poised to fly off their stems.

"They're lovely," I said, and looked up at Bryce

51

gratefully. Bryce put his hand under my hair and caressed my neck. A moment later he was kissing me. I pulled away, frightened at his urgency and my own response. For a moment I sensed Jess's presence. I had moved into her parents' home, even into her room. I was caring for her son and now her husband was making love to me. I felt her anger, and I was afraid she would punish me. "Bryce, I have to go back. I shouldn't be here at all," I managed to say.

Careful not to touch me again, he took me to one of the paths that led to the cabins. "Look, let me see Matt just once. We could meet on the sand dunes tonight after the children's supper. The club members will be eating. All I want is ten minutes with him. What harm can that do?"

I thought of Bryce's tenderness with the orchids and of all the hidden things he could show Matt. "All right," I said. "But just for ten minutes." He smiled and kissed the top of my head. In a minute he was out of sight, but Jess stayed. She and Bryce would have explored those woods together, perhaps made love there. I tried to think what she would want and told myself she would want Matt to be happy and that his happiness depended on seeing Bryce.

On my way back to the Larimers' cabin, someone called my name. I looked up to see Mrs. Bradford waving to me from her porch. "Anne, come in out of that sun and have a cool glass of lemonade with me. I've been wanting to get to know you. The Larimers have such nice things to say about you." She patted the cushion on one of the wicker chairs. Unlike the other wives at the Beaches, Margot Bradford seemed to take little interest in the way her cabin looked. There were no planters filled with flowers on the porch and the wicker was peeling, its cushions faded and water stained. It looked as though she had stopped caring about the Beaches.

It always makes me nervous when someone says they want to get to know me. Mrs. Bradford was certainly friendly, but there was something about her that made me uncomfortable, and I found myself sitting on the edge of my chair.

"We're all one big happy family here," she said, but there was an edge of sarcasm to her voice, and something else. Her words were slurred as though she had been drinking. Then I remembered Dr. Bradford saying he was giving his wife tranquilizers because of something connected with Jess's death. Of course, she was Jess's aunt. Still, I couldn't understand why she would continue to be that upset. It had been nearly a year since Jess died. "How are you getting along with Matt?" Mrs. Bradford asked.

"Fine, I think. He's easy to take care of." She left me to go into the cabin. When she came out she had a plate of store cookies and two glasses of pale lemonade. She handed me mine and set hers on a table beside her and then never touched it. "I want to talk to you about Matt. He's a quiet boy, isn't he? But then he has a lot to think about. His life hasn't been a happy one."

"I think he misses his father," I said. I said it deliberately, hoping to find out why Matt wasn't allowed to see Bryce.

I was unprepared for Mrs. Bradford's reaction. Her face went dead white. "I love the Larimers dearly but I have to tell you they have no business bringing Matt to the Beaches. It's selfish and it's terribly dangerous for Matt."

"I don't understand," I said. "Why is it dangerous?"

She looked to see if anyone was on the boardwalk. There wasn't, but still she lowered her voice. "Because the same thing could happen to Matt." Then she smiled nervously. "I mean Lakeville is so close. Matt's memories can't be pleasant ones."

"But everyone is so good to Matt, and the Beaches is such a beautiful place," I said. We were looking out over the lake. A hatch of fishflies so small you could hardly see them was making the air over the lake vibrate. Down the beach a little way the children were having their sailing lesson. The small boats with their bright crayon-colored sails skimmed over the water like toys.

"Yes," she said, "it's beautiful, but it's not innocent."

I thought a lack of innocence was a strange accusation to make against the Beaches. Did she mean there was too much drinking or perhaps even affairs between members? I wanted to ask, but before I could say anything, Mrs. Bradford surprised me by changing the subject.

"You remind me of Jess," she said. "She was always

too artless, too trusting, for her own good." Jess again, I thought. I couldn't escape her. Suddenly, like a child tired of a toy, she dismissed me. "Run along," she said. "I'm afraid you caught me in a depressed mood. I'm sure everything will be fine."

I was relieved to be dismissed but unsettled by what she seemed to be suggesting.

As I walked away from the Bradfords' cabin Matt came running up from the beach. "I righted the boat all by myself!" he shouted. His face was shining with pride. It was the first time I had seen him so animated, and I began to have doubts about our meeting that evening with Bryce. Perhaps if Matt were just left alone he would in time adjust to the Beaches and forget about Bryce. But what about Bryce? I asked myself. Jess was gone and what else did Bryce have except Matt?

Before dinner I let Matt know we were going to see his father. "I'll tell him all about yesterday's fishing trip," Matt said. "And how I righted the boat. I saw a snake that was bright green. He'll know what it was." Matt was so excited I had to warn him not to give himself away. As usual, Ed and Robin sat at our table. Ed was complaining about the next day's nature walk. "I've dragged these kids around to every hornet's nest and beaver lodge on the place. I don't know what's left. Maybe I'll take them into Lakeville and show them the bar—it doesn't get any wilder than that."

Without thinking, I said, "I know a wonderful place. A hidden bog back behind Grass Lake." I told Ed how to find it. "There are all kinds of plants there," I said. "Sundews, pitcher plants, even orchids." The minute I spoke I regretted it. What if Ed found out how I had happened on the bog? But in his relief all he could think of was how grateful he was to me.

"You've saved my life," Ed said. He gave me a hug. Since our night in Lakeville I had been keeping some distance between us. I was sure Ed noticed and was hurt. Now he was pleased that we'd be doing something together. "Tomorrow you're the resident nature person. And I hope the bog's deep enough to drown Robin." Robin looked up from his dinner and grinned, happy to be mentioned in any context.

8

The sand dunes are misleading. As you approach the leeward side of the lake, the dunes appear to rise up in a gentle slope. There are shrubs and trees to break the line of their rising. It is only when you begin to climb the face of the dunes that you feel the steepness and see how far away the crest is. Matt and I scrambled up the dune that faced the Beaches, laughing, racing each other, pausing breathless, hurrying on, pulling ourselves up by the branches of the stunted shrubs and the dwarfed, scrubby trees that struggled to grow in the sand, until we reached the crown of the dune. Before us, hundreds of feet below, was the lake, a muted blue-green in the early evening light. From our height the large cabins at the Beaches looked like playhouses. The lake was remote and the waves nothing more than faint white scrawls. At the bottom of the dune's windward side we saw Bryce waving to us. Matt and I slid down the dune, avoiding the tufts of sharp beach grass, feeling the uncertainty of the loose sand falling away under our feet. It was as if the whole world were giving way.

When we reached the bottom we threw ourselves onto the warm sand, panting and laughing. While I was still catching my breath, Matt was running toward Bryce. Bryce helped Matt search out smooth flat stones to skip, showing him how to hold them in his hand. The stones leapfrogged over the water. Seeing Matt and Bryce's pleasure in each other's company, I told myself I had been right to bring them together.

I sat on the beach, watching. Matt called to me to be sure I saw how well he was doing. "That's four skips, Annie!" After a while, Bryce said something to Matt and he went off slowly to climb the next dune. Bryce came over to me. Later Matt told me Bryce ordered him to leave us. Matt's back was toward me, so I didn't see the hurt and disappointment on his face at being sent away.

Bryce put his hands on either side of my face and turned it up toward him. He leaned down and kissed me. I pulled away guiltily and looked around at Matt, afraid he might have seen us. At first I couldn't find him. Then Bryce pointed to the top of the dune. There was a small, almost invisible figure waving to us. I was relieved. From that distance he would probably not have recognized Bryce's gesture. Then my relief turned to alarm as I realized how far from me Matt was.

"He's fine," Bryce said, pulling me down beside him on sand still warm from the afternoon sun. "Don't baby him. He gets enough of that at the Beaches."

"He's doing much better," I said. I told Bryce how Matt was beginning to enjoy sailing. "And he's making friends." I thought Bryce would be pleased, but instead he looked angry.

"I don't like what they're doing to Matt. I don't want him to turn into one of them."

For a moment I was annoyed with Bryce for preferring that Matt be unhappy rather than adjust to the Beaches. Then I remembered Bryce's father and Jess and how Bryce wasn't welcome at the Beaches or allowed to see Matt. Of course he would be angry. Anyone would.

I tried to think of something that might please him. "Guess what we're going to do tomorrow," I said. Bryce looked at me. His look said he was beyond playing games. I flushed. "Well, I just wanted you to know that I liked the bog you took me to see so much, we're taking some of the children there." I had thought he wanted the members of the Beaches to learn to appreciate what they had.

Instead he was furious. "I showed it to you. I didn't mean for you to drag a bunch of stupid kids there and spoil it! What in hell were you thinking of?" His face was red with anger, his eyes were narrowed, his fists clenched. I was frightened and suddenly afraid of being there alone with him. I looked around for Matt and was relieved to see he was climbing down the dune. I remembered Mrs. Bradford's alarm when I mentioned Bryce. I was sure there were things about Bryce that Mrs. Larimer had not told me. At that moment all I wanted was to take Matt and get away from Bryce as quickly as possible.

"I'm sorry," I said. "I guess I didn't think you'd mind."

"I don't want you to take them there."

"But it's too late. I've already told them about it, even where it is. They could find it now without me. I'll tell them to be careful." And then, because I was hurt by his unexpected outburst, I said, "Anyhow, it belongs to them."

Bryce jumped up. "Just because they put a fence around everything and hire some stooge security man to keep me from seeing my son doesn't mean anything. This place belongs to the person who knows it best and that's me."

Matt had finished his climb down from the dune and was walking toward us, a frightened look on his face. "What's wrong?" he asked. "What are you fighting about?"

His face had the white, pinched look I remembered from the days when I had begun baby-sitting for him. "We're not fighting," I said. "Everything's all right." But Bryce was striding angrily away from us, and Matt didn't believe me.

"Did my dad hit you?" he asked.

Matt's question took my breath away. For the first time I began to see what I had risked. "Why did you ask me that?" I said. "Did your father ever hurt your mother?" But Matt was running back toward the Beaches.

The next morning at breakfast I tried to discourage Ed from taking the children to the bog. "It's really mushy. One of the kids could fall through. And there were a lot of flies and mosquitoes."

"Keep talking," Ed said. "The more you don't want to go, the more interesting it gets."

Matt coaxed, "Come on, Annie. You said we could go."

"I know," Robin said, "there's a bog monster you don't want us to see." His mouth was full of French toast, and syrup was dripping down his chin.

"I wish you wouldn't talk with your mouth full," Ed said. "In which case we would have total silence from you." He looked at me. "What's the matter, Annie? You look a little down."

"It's probably her time of the month," Robin said. Susan and Meredith giggled.

Ed reached across the table and picked up Robin's glass of milk. Deliberately he poured it over Robin's head. "What a slob," he said to Robin, who for once was too shocked to say anything. "You've got milk all over your clothes. Get back to the cabin and change and be back here in five minutes or I'll tow you out to the middle of the lake and drop you in." He turned to me. "Listen, I can take the kids. You don't have to go."

"I'll help," Matt said. "I've read about bogs."

"I'll go with you," I told Ed. "I have to be sure we're careful. We ought to take as few people as possible. The footsteps you make in that moss don't go away."

"Here she is . . . Miss Ecology," Ed sang. "God, you're getting pompous." But I could see he was pleased I would be going.

Syrie said, "Terry and I will very unselfishly volunteer to give up wet shoes and mosquito bites and suffer through a whole hour without these two brats. I'm sure the other keepers will be willing to make the same sacrifice."

There were twelve of us. Ed and I were the only keepers. When we had climbed down the bank, I called everyone together and warned them, "You've got to watch where you walk. Don't step on any plants, and keep an eye out for holes in the moss. You could go right through." Most of the children were listening carefully to me, a little awed by the seriousness of my voice. Only Robin was off by himself, slapping at dragonflies.

"Annie, you're sounding too environmental for words," Ed said. "I mean, is it all right to breathe the air? Robin, those dragonflies won't bite."

"There're black flies, too." He was still sulking over what had happened at breakfast.

"Flies aren't going to bite you either. Do you think they want to poison themselves? Come on, kids, tippy-toes."

I pointed out the bog plants Bryce had shown me. "The sundews and pitcher plants are carnivorous," I told them, proud of my new knowledge. Matt was fascinated by the sundews. "It's like they have glass Christmas tree ornaments hanging on them."

Robin gave all his attention to the pitcher plants. "Gross," he said. "There are insect arms and legs in their throats."

The children were hushed in the presence of these strange, unfamiliar plants. Feeling the quaking raft under their feet, they moved carefully, taking their cues from us. Only Robin was distracted. When he called out, "Hey, I'm feeding a fly to the pitcher plant," and no one noticed, he looked for some other way to draw attention to himself. We constantly had to remind him to stay on the path. Ed didn't let Robin get away with much, not because he thought Robin stupid and foolish but because he didn't. In spite of his hassling Robin, he liked him. Ed believed Robin could control his clowning if he wanted to.

We were halfway around the bog and had just come to the orchids. I was explaining to the children how rare the orchids were. Matt was bent over the tiny flowers, lost in wonder at their delicacy. "Ouch!" Robin shouted. "I stuck my finger in a pitcher plant and it bit me!" He was shaking his hand and jumping up and down. All of a sudden he fell through the moss and was up to his armpits in black water, struggling to keep his footing.

"Just stick your arms out and tread water," Ed called. "We'll get you out."

Robin continued to thrash around, opening more spaces in the moss and deepening the hole so that he sank even lower. Ed finally managed to calm Robin down. Then, stretching his own body out to distribute its weight, Ed pulled Robin onto firmer ground. Robin was crying, and furious with us for seeing him cry. Walking back to the lodge, the other children, angry with Robin for spoiling their trip, maintained a sulky silence.

Matt walked next to me. "Can we come back here again, Annie? Just the two of us to see the orchids?" he asked.

"I don't know," I said uncertainly. I was afraid Bryce would see the damage we had done to the bog.

As irritated as we were with Robin, at lunch our distaste was softened by the sight of him toying with his food when we were used to his gulping everything down and then helping himself to leftovers on the plates of others. Matt even offered him part of his strawberry pie, which Robin almost accepted until he remembered that he was supposed to be too miserable to eat. He wouldn't talk to any of us.

I thought he would be all right in a few hours, but he stayed away from the cookout that evening. The cookout was a Beaches tradition. Once each summer the club members had a lobster boil on the beach with the children. A large grill was set up. Dr. Bradford was

presiding in a chef's hat and big white apron that said
THE BEACHES. Boiling away on the grill were two im-
mense pots, one filled with corn and the other with
lobsters that had been flown in from the East Coast.

Matt was running around with the other children in
that aimless way children do when they are excited and
waiting for something to happen. I remembered how
withdrawn Matt had been when I first started baby-sitting. Nothing interested him then but television, and
it made no difference what he watched—game shows,
soaps, anything as long as there was sound and something moved on the screen. Mrs. Larimer was watching
Matt, too, and must have been thinking the same thing,
because she put her arm around me, right in front of all
the other people, and said, "We really lucked out when
we found Anne."

Of course I felt guilty about Bryce, but after his outburst the night before, I had decided that neither Matt
nor I would meet Bryce again.

The dinner was delicious. We all ended up with but-
ter running down our chins. Jokes went around about
past cookouts, but by now some of those stories were
familiar to me and I didn't feel as left out. The adults
sat around the campfire in a circle with the children
making up an inner circle. Syrie and Terry and some of
the other keepers had come over to sit with me and for
the first time I felt as though I belonged.

At the edge of the lake a huge orange sun was bal-
anced on the line of the horizon. "Who'll be the first

one to see the green flash?" Mr. Larimer called out. You were supposed to see the flash a second before the sun set. The green flash was half mirage and half legend. As the sun disappeared there were shouts of "I saw it!" But no one could agree on when it had happened. Matt had been one of those to cry out and now Meredith and then some of the other keepers and the Bradfords were saying, "Matt was the one to see it." Mrs. Bradford was almost shrill in the insistent way she was calling out. Ever since I had come to the Beaches I had been aware of how everyone went out of their way to be kind to Matt. It was not just his mother's death, but something more than that. The club members were not only sympathetic; they seemed to have some sort of vested interest in Matt—and in his happiness—like parents who have made an enormous sacrifice for a child and are anxious to see him succeed.

It was growing dark and the bonfire was lit. The children had been gathering driftwood all week, and now as the towering pile exploded into flames that leapt high into the dark sky, they shouted and danced around the fire. In the red glare the dancing figures looked like animated cave paintings. The parents must have seen something too primitive in their children's behavior because they set about calming them down. Ed was called upon to distribute marshmallows and green sticks, and the children began jockeying for space around the fire. There were cries of "ukulele" and Mr. Clements, a retired judge, produced one and began strumming on it. Everyone joined in the singing. The Clementses were favorites. They were in their eighties but they were on the tennis courts every morning. Their cabin was always filled with children—grandchildren and great-grandchildren—and it was rumored that they still went skinny-dipping.

The songs were ones I remembered my father singing on car trips when I was very young: "Someone's in the Kitchen with Dinah" and "Under the Bamboo Tree"— foolish, nostalgic songs. Thinking of how far away my dad was, I felt tears in my eyes and was glad of the darkness and the smoke from the fire that would be my excuse if anyone noticed.

Luckily no one seemed to be looking my way. They were all concentrating on the singing and the bonfire. All except Mrs. Bradford, who was staring past everyone out toward the dark lake. A look of resentment, like a mask, was frozen on her face. She hates these people, I thought, but I couldn't imagine why.

There was another tradition. As the bonfire burned down, candles were brought out and one by one we each lit one. Then in silence we began walking home. All along the boardwalk you could see the small flickering lights moving through the darkness. The Larimers were just ahead of me, and Matt walked between them. Mrs. Larimer looked over her shoulder and saw that I was alone. She motioned for her husband and Matt to wait until I caught up with them and then, signaling Matt to go on ahead with his grandfather, put her arm in mine and we walked back together.

9

When Matt and I went over to the lodge for breakfast the next morning, there was a new feeling of closeness between us. The evening had been a turning point. Both of us were happier, more at peace at the Beaches: both of us had left something upsetting a little further behind. Thomas was already down on the beach clearing away the charred remains of the bonfire. The sky was hazy and you could barely tell the difference between the lake and the horizon.

As we got closer to the lodge we were startled by shouts. Several of the children and their keepers were gathered at the door of the lodge. Ed was there with Robin. It was Robin who was shouting. "I didn't do it!"

he was screaming. "I didn't do it!" The steps of the lodge were strewn with wilted foliage. I guessed that Robin, as a prank, had pulled up some plants from the flower beds around the lodge. When I looked more closely I saw that the flowers were the wild orchids from the bog. They had been uprooted and left to die on the lodge porch. I felt as though I were witnessing a murder. Matt reached for my hand. Ed was quiet, staring at Robin. "You were the only one who wasn't at the cookout last night," Syrie said to Robin. "Who else had a chance to do it?"

"I was just in my room. I was sick of people always yelling at me."

All Ed said was, "Let's get out of here." He dragged Robin back toward the Beamish cabin.

At breakfast everyone wanted to talk about the cookout. As far as they were concerned, pulling up the orchids was just one of Robin's sick jokes. None of them seemed to realize how special and rare the orchids were. I wasn't surprised that Robin had denied he had done it. He was not the kind of child who would stand up bravely and confess to doing something wrong. But neither Matt nor I thought Robin was malicious. Matt had whispered to me, "I believe him." I wasn't sure.

It was too early for Matt's tennis lesson, so after breakfast we went down to the beach to skip stones. Matt was practicing regularly since Bryce had shown him how. It was something he was better at than many of the older boys. Thomas was collecting the last charred embers of the bonfire in his garden cart. "What was all that hollering at the lodge?" he asked me. I was startled to have him say anything to me at all, much less ask me a question. He always seemed so indifferent to what went on at the Beaches.

"Robin Beamish was upset. They think he pulled up some rare orchids from the bog back near Grass Lake."

"That boy is a mess, but he didn't pull up those plants."

"Who did then?" But Thomas was wheeling the cart away.

Ed and I had arranged to meet for coffee in the lodge while Matt and Robin had their tennis lessons. He was there ahead of me. "How is Robin?" I asked.

"He's mad as hell at being accused of tearing up those plants. It's not that whining stuff I get when I call him on cheating. He's really indignant."

"Thomas said Robin didn't do it."

Ed looked surprised. "He actually volunteered that? To tell you the truth, I don't believe Robin did it either. I think it's a bum rap, but his parents are furious. His aunt is a grade-one eco nut. She claims Robin is cursed with original eco sin inherited from his father the developer. Robin is plenty loathsome but he's not wicked. If he didn't do it, though, who did?"

"What will they do to Robin?"

"The Woods and Waters Committee is meeting this afternoon. What a name for a committee. It sounds like God should chair it. They'll probably ask Robin for some kind of written apology, which will be tough, first of all because I'm not sure he can write and secondly because he's such a stubborn bastard I don't think he'll admit to doing it."

"What will happen then?"

"I think his folks are fed up with him. They're talking about sending him to a fat camp or a computer camp for the rest of the summer."

"You'd lose your job then."

"Yes, and I need the money, or believe me, I wouldn't be playing nursemaid to Robin."

I didn't want to go through the rest of the summer without Ed. Although I was beginning to feel I belonged, I could talk about the Beaches more honestly with him than with anyone else. "I'd hate to see you go," I said.

"I'll come back and take you for rides to the Dairy Queen." He was grinning, but I could tell he was pleased by my saying I would miss him.

By dinnertime Robin and Ed were gone. "Mr. Beamish was driving back today anyhow, so he just decided to take Robin with him," Syrie said. "Good riddance as far as I'm concerned. That child is a real pill." Matt didn't say anything.

"What about Ed?" I asked.

"He went home," Meredith said. She looked unhappy and I noticed that she wasn't wearing the mascara she usually sneaked from Terry to impress Ed. Matt noticed too. "How come no raccoon eyes tonight?" he asked.

"Shut up, Matt," Meredith said. "Eating with babies is a real drag."

Squabbles between Matt and Meredith were rare. Meredith usually assumed a protective role with Matt, seeing that he wasn't left out of things. The destruction of the orchids had made us all edgy.

Coming back from the lodge, we met the Larimers on their way to dinner. "Ed left a note for you, Anne," Mrs. Larimer said. She smiled knowingly. The Larimers had often seen me with Ed. "It's with your mail on the hall table."

The other keepers all looked forward to their mail— it was one of the highlights of the day. "How else are we supposed to know there's still a real world out there?" Syrie had said, making for the mailbox at the entrance gate to the club. I was less eager for letters, which were usually from my mother and filled with forced cheerfulness and suppressed rage. All week long I would work at forgetting what had happened to my parents and then a letter would come and it would be as though I was hearing about their divorce for the first time.

I picked up Ed's note along with a letter from my mother and another envelope on which my name and address had been typed and went out on the porch to be alone while I read them. Matt was inside watching a *M.A.S.H.* rerun. I put my mother's letter aside and opened the note from Ed.

> *Dear Annie,*
> *Not to worry. The Beamishes finally re-*

*alized what I was putting up with and paid
me off for the whole summer—"Combat
pay," Mr. Beamish said. So I have the
money and I don't have to put up with the
Grub. Although to be fair I still don't think
Robin was responsible. The best thing about
the Beaches was getting to know you—even
if you come from a place that's actually called
Colonial Gardens. I'll be in touch.*

Love, Ed

When I finished Ed's note, I started to open the second envelope. It was stamped but there was something
odd about the look of the letter. I realized there was no
postmark and the lines drawn through the stamp had
been made by hand to look like a cancellation.

Inside the envelope was a single sheet of paper. When
I unfolded it something dropped out. I reached down to
pick it up. It was one of the orchids, crumpled, the
stem limp, the dried-out flower looking as though it had
been fashioned from lavender tissue paper. I read the
note: THIS IS THE LAST THING THE BEACHES WILL TAKE
AWAY FROM ME.

There was no signature but I knew it was from Bryce.

My first impulse was to let Ed and Matt and the
Beamishes and everyone else at the Beaches know that
Robin was innocent, that he should never have been
sent away. But how would I explain how I knew who
had done it? If I said Bryce had told me, they would

immediately ask why he was writing letters to me. I would have to explain about Bryce's meetings with Matt. The Larimers would be furious, and like Ed, I would be sent away, only I would be sent away in disgrace. And there was something else. What would Matt think of having a father who would do something so outrageous, so malicious? As it was, Matt had very little to hang on to. He would be depressed all over again. I knew I wouldn't do anything about the letter and suddenly I hated Bryce for making me underhanded and deceitful.

IO

In the days that followed, Matt spent less time with me. He and Lance Brightman were making a tree house at the edge of the woods. I tried not to get in their way, but now that I knew what Bryce was capable of, I wasn't letting Matt out of my sight. I sat nearby, reading while the boys dragged planks of driftwood up into the tree and hammered away. Matt put up with my watching him. Lance's keeper was his cousin Bing Roberts, the sailing instructor. Bing had agreed to take care of his cousin, but he was only too glad to leave Lance for hours—even though it was against club rules—knowing I'd keep an eye on both boys. Lance, used to more freedom, complained to Matt about me. "How can you stand having that girl around all the time?"

Matt shrugged the question off. "She's not so bad."

Someone else had taken an interest in Matt. One afternoon when Lance was off with his parents and sister on a trip to Mackinac Island, Matt and I were sitting on the Larimers' porch. I was writing letters and Matt was building a house for a small toad he had rescued from a garter snake. The toad was half in the snake's mouth when we had come upon it. Matt had made a dash for the snake and grabbed it, shaking the toad loose. He had thrown the snake into the woods and picked up the toad, who was immobilized by fright. "He needs to be safe for a while," Matt said, and brought the toad home. He was furnishing the toad's house with small stones and twigs and building a little mound of dirt in one corner. He'd already put two dead flies and a dead grasshopper in the box and was tacking a screen over the top.

Neither of us heard Thomas approach. He had a fishing pole in his hand. "I made you something," he said to Matt. Matt jumped up eagerly, nearly upsetting the toad's box.

"It's beautiful," Matt said. He showed it proudly to me. The rod was made of split bamboo and tapered to almost nothing. I thought it looked more like some sort of fairy wand than a rod that would support a fighting fish.

"It's for fly-fishing," Thomas said.

"But I don't know how to fly-fish. My dad never showed me that kind of fishing."

"I can show you," Thomas said.

I supposed Bryce had not taught Matt fly-fishing because it was a kind of cult at the Beaches. The Sandy River, which ran along the eastern border of the club, was known all over the state for its trout fishing. First thing every morning and every evening after dinner, you saw at least one of the men setting off for some fishing, lugging his waders and fly rod. They seldom took creels because it was considered poor form to keep any trout. Most of them fished without barbs on their hooks. Ed had jokingly told me that it was a kind of genteel cover for not being able to catch fish.

Once in a great while one of the members would talk Thomas into guiding for him. Then they would drive to one of the dirt trails that led to the stream, put in their canoe, and float down while Thomas told the member where to cast. Under Thomas's instruction he would catch trout, but Thomas was reluctant to act as a guide even when someone tried to bribe him with money or time off from his maintenance job. After being turned down by Thomas, Dr. Bradford said, "He doesn't think we ought to take fish out of that stream. He thinks they're *his fish.*"

That was why it was all the more surprising that Thomas had made the fishing rod for Matt. The Larimers were as amazed as I was. "You've made a real friend," Mr. Larimer told Matt. "I'd give several hundred dollars for a rod like this in my size. If you keep on Thomas's good side you'll turn into the best fisherman around here,

although to tell you the truth, that's not saying a lot."
The Larimers seemed much happier than they had at
the start of the season. Mrs. Larimer was more relaxed.
She was going into Blue Harbor to have her hair done
each week and was playing golf at the Blue Harbor Club
with some of the other women at the Beaches.

The next afternoon Thomas stopped by for us. We
got into his old truck and drove a quarter of a mile or
so before we cut into a two track that led down to the
river. There was a sandy spit sticking out into the water.
"It's a good place to learn," Thomas said. "No trees."
He had brought a net and a creel and a small plastic
box into which he had put artificial flies and a tin
of some sort of wax. He handed Matt the wax and
said, "You got to grease your line so it floats on the
water. That way they can't see it. We got to fool the
trout."

I wandered off a little way to look at the river. It was
wide at that point, edged by grassy banks and bright
with the sun that caught the riffles and lit the river
bottom. Looking down into the clear river was like
looking through the glass of a shop window; the bright
river stones might be for sale. Upstream the river was
very different. It narrowed through a cedar swamp, and
the banks were crisscrossed with the fallen spars of ce-
dars. The swamp looked dark and menacing.

Matt was absorbed in watching Thomas cast. His line
snapped upstream fifty feet and more to land light as a
fallen leaf on the water. On his second cast Thomas

hooked a good-sized trout. I ran back to look at it. It was flopping on the grass and the iridescent colors along its belly shimmered in the sun.

"Are you going to throw it back?" Matt asked.

"We'll keep it. There's nothing wrong with knowing how to get your food someplace else besides a supermarket."

"I'm going to look around," I said, but they were so absorbed in their fishing, I don't think either Matt or Thomas heard me. I headed downstream, following a bend in the river for half a mile or so, stopping at a meadow thick with blueberry bushes. It was my first experience with wild berries, and I had the city person's greed for something free. They were low bush berries and I had to stoop over to pick them. There was a cool breeze off the river, and the sun beating down on my back felt good. I had never seen wild blueberries before and I was delighted with the variety of colors—all on the same shrub—frosted shades of green, pink, lavender, purple, and black.

As I picked I noticed footprints in the sandy soil like those of a barefoot boy, and I supposed someone had been there before me. Whoever it was had been reckless in their picking, for whole patches of berry bushes had been trampled. A rustling noise and a kind of whine made me straighten up. There, the length of a room from me, stood a mother bear with her cub. Though I knew very little about the woods, even I knew a mother bear protecting her cub was dangerous. There were no trees to climb and even if there were, I didn't know how to climb trees and bears did. We looked at each other. She seemed enormous to me, hundreds of pounds, with black shaggy fur and small black piggish eyes. The cub was whimpering. I was trembling all over and terrified that I might pass out from fright. The bear swung her head away from me, listening. Someone was striding toward us. At the sound of the approaching footsteps, the bear made a kind of "woof" at her cub and began lumbering off, swinging her head and body. The cub scampered along after her.

I looked gratefully in the direction of the footsteps, ready to thank Thomas for rescuing me. But it wasn't Thomas, it was Bryce. In my relief I blurted, "I just saw a bear and her cub!"

He paid no attention to what I said or how upset I was. "What's Thomas doing with Matt!"

It was an accusation and not a question. "He's teaching Matt to fly-fish."

"That's my responsibility, not his. I don't want any dirty Indian hanging around my son."

"That's not fair. He just wants to be nice to Matt." I backed away from him. I had just remembered the orchids.

"What's not fair is that I can't have a chance to go fishing with my own boy." Suddenly Bryce's voice became soft. "I'm sorry about the orchids, Annie. I guess I just got carried away. I thought that place I showed you was just between the two of us, and then you handed it over to the Beaches as if it didn't mean anything to you."

There was some truth in what Bryce was telling me, but it didn't justify what he had done.

"Look, I know I'm not doing myself or Matt any good by staying around here. I spend every day trying to figure out where Matt is. I've got to get on with my life, even if it means leaving Matt. Maybe one day things will change and I'll be able to see him again. In the meantime, I'm taking off."

Standing there shielding his blue eyes from the sun, his shoulders slightly stooped as though he were self-conscious about his height, Bryce seemed so vulnerable I almost felt sorry for him. I wasn't sure it was fair that he should be driven from his own town and away, perhaps forever, from Matt. I tried to think of something I could do to make it easier for him. "If you want to send me your address," I said, "I could write to you. I'll probably be baby-sitting with Matt downstate, too. I can tell you how he's doing."

"Yeah, well, that would be nice. I'd appreciate that. But there's just one favor I want to ask you. I'll be leaving next week. I've already started to pack. I want to see Matt one time before I leave. I don't want him to think I ran out on him. I'll check the tree at Grass Lake each morning next week."

"I couldn't let Matt see you again. It wouldn't be fair to the Larimers."

"You haven't told them about our meetings?"

"No. They would be furious with me." The minute the words were out of my mouth I saw how foolish I had been. Now Bryce knew he had a weapon to use against me. He was smiling. "You keep an eye on the tree. I'll let you know just before I'm ready to leave," he said, "and you can bring Matt to say good-bye to me." He was threatening me: let me see Matt or I let the Larimers know about our meetings.

Before I could say a word, Bryce had turned his back and was walking away. I considered making some excuse to the Larimers, telling them I had heard from my mother and was needed at home. I suddenly wanted to get away from Bryce and Matt and the Beaches. But I knew I couldn't leave Matt without warning the Larimers about Bryce, and there was no way I could do that without exposing my betrayal. There was no one I could turn to. My father was far away and I couldn't forgive him for leaving my mom and me. I thought of calling or writing my mother, asking her for advice. Then I decided against it. Her letters had grown more depressed and self-absorbed. She was going through enough without my inflicting my own problems on her. I saw that I would have to stay until Bryce was gone. "I'm packing," he had said. I would have just one more week to get through and then Matt and I would be safe. I followed the stream back to Thomas and Matt. They had started loading the truck.

"Where've you been?" Matt wanted to know. "You look like you've seen a ghost."

"More exciting than that," I said. "I ran into a bear and her cub."

"Where were they?" Matt was ready to go in search of them.

"I guess I was trespassing in their blueberry patch. And you don't want to go looking for them, Matt. I've never been so scared in my life."

Thomas grinned. "That sow's been around here for years. I've run into her plenty of times. She won't hurt you. I know where her den is. I could have gone there any winter day and shot her if I had wanted to. I'll tell you a funny thing. A couple of years ago I saw her eating a hornets' nest big as a football. They were buzzing all around her and it never bothered her. She just snapped them up like a dog snapping up a fly." I had never heard Thomas utter that many words all at once. I could see he was enjoying Matt's company.

"Can we go and find the bear?" Matt asked.

"Some other time," Thomas said. "They're a little touchy when they have a cub in tow."

Matt insisted on showing me what he had learned. His line only went out a few yards, but it was straight and it landed gently on the water. "You've got fishing in your bones," Thomas said, and I wondered if Thomas was thinking of Bryce's father.

"Can we take my grandmother's station wagon and come here and practice?" Matt asked me.

"No," I said too quickly. I wasn't going to risk having

Matt meet Bryce. "No, there are places we can practice closer to the Beaches."

"But there are too many trees. I'll get my line snagged in the branches. Why can't we practice right here?"

Thomas had been watching me. "You can practice on the landing," he said. The landing was a quarter of a mile upstream from where the river emptied into Lake Michigan. When the members fished in canoes, it was where they got out. "Annie, she doesn't want to run into any more big bears in the woods," Thomas said, and gave me a shrewd look.

That afternoon Mr. Larimer sent me over to the Bradfords' cabin. "Ask Dr. Bradford if he has a couple of bottles of tonic water to spare. We're having a small cocktail party tonight and we're running low. I swore I wouldn't get caught short this summer, but they're even drinking it with rum. And a lime, too. Thanks, Anne."

It was the middle of July and the hot sun was beating down on the boardwalk. I decided to take the shaded path along the back of the cabins, a path that was seldom used, except by the maintenance people.

Approaching the Bradfords' cabin, I could hear voices raised in an argument. "It was a Beaches' decision, Margot, not my decision." Dr. Bradford sounded impatient, like a parent who has explained things again and again to a child.

"I won't have a club making my decisions, Don. You've grown up with them deciding your life. I'm sick of that. Summer after summer I've been stuck up here with your relatives and your friends. I've had summer after summer of bridge and tennis and mindless chatter."

"Why didn't you tell me you felt that way, Margot? I thought you liked the club."

"I came because it meant so much to you. I know you wanted it for the children. But I'm not letting the Beaches decide what is right and wrong for me."

"Stop thinking about yourself, Margot, and think about Matt. What kind of life do you want him to have?"

"What kind of life will he have if it's based on lies?"

"What would it be like if he knew the truth? It would be a horror."

"But suppose Bryce comes back."

"He won't. He knows better than to come here. And that girl, Anne, is very trustworthy. I've been noticing lately how conscientious she is about keeping an eye on Matt."

"Why should Bryce be afraid to try to see Matt? He has as much on the Beaches as we have on him."

"Margot, you know that's not true. Where is your sense of proportion?"

Hearing Matt's name, I had purposely eavesdropped. But the conversation hadn't answered my questions, only raised new ones and made me more determined than ever that Bryce shouldn't see Matt again. By the time I walked noisily up the porch stairs the voices were silent.

II

All the keepers had Saturday nights and Sunday afternoons off. On Saturday morning Ed called me. "I've got something interesting to tell you. How about getting together tonight? I'll pick you up and we can drive into Blue Harbor—it's more your style than Lakeville."

I was still feeling guilty about Robin and Ed having to leave the Beaches, so I was glad to have a chance to see Ed and reassure myself that I hadn't ruined the summer for him. He arrived at the gate of the Beaches in a blue van. ACE HARDWARE, LAKEVILLE was spelled out in large letters on the door. "Sorry it's not a BMW. My dad was going to get one but he couldn't fit the snowplows and wheelbarrows in it," Ed joked.

We were now in Blue Harbor. Gas lamps lit the boutique-lined streets, giving them an old-fashioned look. "I'll treat you to one of those two-dollar ice cream cones. We can take them to the park. What flavor do you want? Tomato zucchini? Whale blubber?"

The park was at the water's edge. A few fishermen still remained on the long pier that stretched out into the lake. In the middle of the park there was a bandshell left over from the days when Saturday-night band concerts were the social event of the week.

We ate our cones and watched the last boats dock and take down their sails. You could smell the scent of phlox and roses from the carefully tended flower beds. "I got a letter from Robin," Ed said. "Luckily they sent him to the computer camp and not the fat camp. He's not doing too badly. Robin's smarter than most people give him credit for. Maybe that's his trouble. I still think the orchid trashing was a bum rap. I'd like to get my hands on whoever is really responsible. But that's not what I wanted to talk to you about. You ought to know that a couple of people in Lakeville have seen Bryce Stevens. I thought about going to the Larimers, but I didn't want to worry them, and anyhow, what happens at the Beaches these days isn't my business anymore. As long as you're careful to keep an eye on Matt, you don't have to worry. I don't believe Bryce would dare go near the Beaches. They're all down on him, although I've never found out why."

"Where is Bryce living?" I asked, making my voice as indifferent as possible.

"I heard he's staying with an old high school buddy of his outside of town. The friend isn't too savory a character, not exactly Bryce's type. Bryce always used to have a certain amount of class. He doesn't seem to be looking for work, so maybe he's just passing through. None of his family lives here any more. His mom moved downstate with Bryce's sister when Bryce's father died. Of course, there's Matt. Do you think the Larimers would let him see Matt?"

"No." I longed to tell Ed the truth. I think I had some fantasy that he would force Bryce out of town. But Ed was too angry about Robin being blamed for something he hadn't done. I didn't see how I could tell him I had known the truth and kept quiet.

"How's Matt doing?" Ed wanted to know.

"Fine. He and Thomas have gotten to be friends."

"Interesting."

"What do you mean?"

"I mean Thomas and Bryce's father used to be thick as thieves when they were both working at the Beaches."

"You told me Bryce's father was fired from the club because he was part of a poaching ring. Are you saying Thomas was too?"

"Just the opposite. There was talk that the poaching got so bad, Thomas got mad and turned Bryce's old man in. Maybe when the old man died Thomas started feeling a little guilty. Now he's trying to make it up by playing granddaddy to Matt."

"How would Bryce feel about that?" I wondered what Ed would say.

"He'd be mad as hell. He hates Thomas's guts."

"Ed, why is Thomas able to get away with so much at the Beaches? He says and does exactly what he wants to."

"They like the novelty of having someone around who doesn't fawn on them."

"They're not like that."

"You used to be more objective."

"I'm more objective than you are."

"I'm probably just envious, but at least I try to look at them realistically. I mean, do you honestly feel you're a part of them? It's like they're some sort of secret society and you and I will never know the password."

Without thinking, I said, "Bryce must have felt that way too."

"You seem to take an interest in him. Maybe you'd like me to arrange an introduction." His voice was bitter.

I tried to reassure him. "I'm just curious. I don't understand why the Larimers dislike him so. They must know something about him that we don't know, something that makes them keep Matt away from him."

"You've got it the wrong way around. Bryce kept Jess and Matt away from the Beaches. Turnabout is fair play. Anyhow I'm tired of talking about the Beaches. Let's get out of here. This place is spooky when it's deserted."

The fishermen were gone. The only people left in the park were an elderly man walking a small plump dog that bounced across the lawn like a ball, and two listless teenagers. "I really appreciate your warning me, Ed."

I realized the evening had not gone the way Ed had hoped. Maybe telling me about Bryce had just been an excuse to see me. And then I had spent the whole evening talking about Bryce and the Beaches. We walked back along the deserted streets to the van. Ed helped me up the high step and got in himself. He turned the key to start the engine. Nothing happened. He tried again. "It can't be the battery," he said. "We just put a new one in." He got out of the van and looked under the hood. I heard him swear. "It's the battery all right. Some bastard stole it! That's what we get for coming to a ritzy town like Blue Harbor. In Lakeville no one would do a thing like that."

I remembered the way Bryce had suddenly appeared by the river when Matt and Thomas and I were there, how he seemed always to be watching. I wondered if I was getting paranoid. "What will you do?" I asked.

"There's a filling station that's open about a mile from here. I'll get a rebuilt battery, but my dad's going to be pissed. You can wait here in the van. I won't be long."

"No," I said quickly. "I'll go with you."

Ed was pleased. He thought I was going because I wanted to be with him.

It was nearly midnight when we got back to the Beaches. Ed parked the van at the entrance and I took out my key for the heavy lock that hung from the gate. "You know your way from here," Ed said. "I'd better be getting back and break the bad news to my dad."

I kissed him good night. "Why don't you come over for the canoe race this week?"

"Back to Bryce again."

"What do you mean?"

"Didn't you know he used to race every year when he lived in Lakeville?"

"How would I know that?"

"Sorry, I didn't mean to hassle you. I'll be there."

I listened to Ed's van drive away. I knew Bryce couldn't be everywhere. He couldn't be in Lakeville and in Blue Harbor and here at the Beaches. Yet I sensed his presence. He doesn't have to be here, I thought. He's become a part of me; I carry him around. That realization was more frightening than having him jump out at me from behind some tree or bush.

12

It was the last week in July and the Beaches was getting ready for the annual Sandy River canoe race. It was exactly the sort of event the club loved. It had tradition, it had to do with the outdoors, and part of it was on their property. The race began at noon in a town far upriver and ended twelve hours later where the Sandy emptied into Lake Michigan, just at the property line of the Beaches. It was the big event for all the small towns in the area and the one night the club opened its gates and invited the local people onto the property. Free soft drinks were handed out to everyone. "A nuisance but good public relations" was the way they referred to it at the club. The competitors in the race came from all over the state. There were articles in the

local newspapers, and the canoes in the race were spon-
sored by the town merchants, who along with the
Beaches chipped in for prizes.

Ed arrived shortly after supper. As soon as it grew
dark Ed and Matt and I joined the others and made our
way along the beach to the mouth of the river. As a
special treat, the children were allowed to stay up for
the midnight finish. We all carried blankets or folding
chairs, and several of the members had elaborate cam-
eras with them. The TV reporters from Blue Harbor
had come to record the arrival of the first canoe.

"My dad used to be in this race," Matt told Ed. I
could see Matt was half hoping Bryce would be racing
that evening. "I could never see him race because it was
at the Beaches."

Ed looked at me but only said, "The whole town of
Lakeville is here. I'm going to hear about hanging out
with the Beaches crowd." He waved self-consciously to
his friends. "Eagletown is here, too," he said. "There's
an Indian crew this year." Some of Ed's friends were
calling out to him. I couldn't hear what they said, but
it made him blush. "Maybe we ought to walk upstream
a way," he said.

"I've got a great idea, Annie," Matt said. "Why don't
you and Ed and I go upstream to the landing? We'll see
the canoes before they get to the finish." Matt and I
had spent several afternoons at the landing while he
practiced his casting. It was only a short walk through
the woods and we had flashlights.

"Go over and ask your grandparents for permission."

I could see the Larimers hesitating for a moment before agreeing. Then Matt and Ed and I moved away from the crowds and into the dark woods. We walked along the path, stepping into the circles of light our flashlights made for one another. I knew there were night animals along the stream—raccoons and beaver. Perhaps they were only a few feet off the trail, watching, curious at the strangers moving through their territory. Suddenly two black shapes appeared on the trail—a doe and her fawn attracted to our lights. The three of us stood still, hardly breathing, waiting to see what the deer would do. They stopped as we had, staring at the lights we held in our hands. Their eyes took fire from the reflection, like the animals' eyes you see burning in the darkness of a roadside. The fawn had come to rest by the side of the doe. It turned its head slightly in her direction to catch any signal of danger. Suddenly the doe broke and ran, the fawn after her. Ed and I turned to each other and laughed with pleasure. Matt was thrilled. "We were so close!" he kept saying.

The trail ended at the landing where the river served as a boundary for the property. We cleared away some twigs and stones and settled down on the bank. It was only minutes before we heard paddles pushing against water and a voice calling "Hup, hup," to mark the rhythm of the paddles' strokes. Matt shone his flashlight on the canoe. Immediately Ed grabbed it out of Matt's hands. We could hear one of the men in the canoe swear. "You're not supposed to do that," Ed said. "It breaks their stroke and it's important that their eyes stay used to the dark."

"But they had a lantern at the end of their boat."

"Yes, but the lantern doesn't shine in their eyes. It shines on the water so they can see stumps and dead-heads."

"Is that canoe going to be the winner?" Matt asked, chastened.

"Probably not," Ed said. "They draw lots to see which canoe goes in the water first and then they subtract the time each canoe has to wait for its start. That canoe may have a low handicap."

A second canoe came gliding through the darkness, the outline of the men just visible in their lantern's faint light. They had headbands and the one in front had stripped off his shirt; you could see the muscles work in his back and arms.

"Went to high school with him," Ed whispered. "The girls think he's a real hunk."

A third canoe was rounding the curve of the river. The paddler in front was calling the strokes. Matt ran to the edge of the river. The canoe was level with us and Matt had his flashlight on again. "Get that damn light out," the man in front called.

"Dad, it's me." Bryce broke his stroke for a second and then plunged his paddle back into the water. There had been a faint smile on his lips as he looked toward the shore, but he didn't say a word. The abrupt illumination of Bryce's face confirmed my worst fear for me.

When I concealed my first meeting with Bryce, I had opened a door that he would enter and reenter. Matt and I would never be free of him. Now it was too late for confessions and nothing else I could think of would work.

"That was my dad," Matt said to us. "Is he going to win?" There was hope and pride in his voice. Several canoes came by, but Matt hardly noticed.

"He has a good chance," Ed said to Matt. "Why don't we go and see?" For an answer Matt jumped up. When Matt was out of hearing, Ed turned to me. "Matt didn't seem all that surprised to see his dad." He was puzzled—and suspicious.

Before I could make up some explanation, the woods ahead of us filled with people and light. It was the Larimers and the Bradfords and several other members sweeping the woods with their flashlights.

"Matt, Anne," Mr. Larimer called, "are you there?" As soon as they saw us they surrounded Matt. Mrs. Larimer put her arm around him and pulled him toward her. "We're taking you back to the cabin," she said.

Matt twisted away. "I don't want to go back. I want to go down and see who won."

Everyone was quiet. Then Dr. Bradford said, "Your father won."

"Well, can't I go and see him?" Matt's voice was excited.

"No," Mr. Larimer said. Just "No"—no other explanation.

Matt was crying with frustration. The months of separation from Bryce that he had never understood, his mother's death, which no one ever mentioned, were suddenly all too much. "You can't keep me away from my father. It's illegal." Coming from a ten-year-old, the word "illegal" was so desperate it silenced everyone.

"Come back to the cabin with us and we'll talk about it tomorrow." Mr. Larimer's voice was firm, almost harsh. I could hear the alarm, but Matt only heard the refusal.

"I won't go. I've got a right to see my dad when he won the race."

Mrs. Larimer said, "Please come back with us, Matt."

Matt didn't move. Finally Mr. Larimer reached down and picked Matt up.

Matt was so surprised that for a minute he didn't react. By the time he began kicking and screaming they were all striding back toward the cabins. Ed and I were left standing alone in the woods.

"What's wrong with those people?" Ed said. "Bryce may be a bastard, but he's Matt's father. Why would it hurt so much for Matt to go down and see his father bask in a little limelight? They carried Matt away like the goddamn KGB. Those people weren't cautious, they were terrified."

But I had started to cry. I had been frightened at the way Bryce had materialized out of the darkness. I wanted to tell the whole story, but after seeing the Larimers' panic I felt more than ever that they would be furious with me if they knew about Matt's meetings with Bryce.

"Hey," Ed said, putting his arms around me, "don't take these weirdos so seriously. Try to keep out of their world. Come on, let's walk you back to the cabin."

When Ed left me at the Larimers', Thomas and Lyle Neeb were out in front with Dr. Bradford. Lyle looked excited and eager, as though he had been given some important mission. Thomas was quiet, and I saw him look over in my direction. Our eyes met and I looked quickly away.

13

Mr. Larimer and Mrs. Bradford were in the living room. Mrs. Bradford was running her hand through her hair, so that it looked disheveled; it was something she did when she was upset. Her face was streaked with tears, a reminder that my own face must look the same way. I started for the stairs. Mr. Larimer called after me, "Anne, would you go up to Matt's room? I think Mrs. Larimer wants to see you."

I stopped to wash my face and try to collect myself and then I went to find Mrs. Larimer. She was just leaving Matt's room and motioned me to be quiet. "Dr. Bradford gave Matt a shot to calm him down and he's asleep now. Mr. Larimer and I have to go next door to the Bradfords' for an hour or so. I want you to stay here and keep an eye on Matt. Lyle is just outside patrolling the house, so there's nothing to worry about." She put a hand on my shoulder. "I know this has been a worry for you, Anne, and it's one you don't need. You have enough to think about these days." She was referring to my parents' divorce. I had no idea she knew about it. Suddenly I realized that she must have done a good deal of checking before she hired me. The thought startled me. I had assumed she had taken me on trust, on the evidence she had seen in my caring for Matt.

After they left for the Bradfords', I looked in Matt's room. He was asleep, one arm flung out, his mouth slightly open. He was so still that I tiptoed into the room and leaned over his bed to be sure he was breathing. When I was reassured that Matt was all right, I went downstairs. From the window I could see Lyle making the rounds of the house. The elaborate precautions seemed absurd and overly dramatic. Why were they so afraid of Bryce? Then I saw something even stranger: circles of light approaching. I watched as the members of the Beaches came down the boardwalk to the Bradfords' cabin: the Robertses, the Thompsons, the Clementses, the Stocktons, the Beamishes, the Duncans, the McKeans, the Parkers, the Brightmans, and the Petersons. With the Larimers and Bradfords already there, the entire club was present. I couldn't imagine what they were doing. For a moment I thought there might be a tradition of having some sort of celebration after the canoe race, but the Latimers surely wouldn't be leaving Matt for some social obligation. It was eerie seeing everyone file into the Bradfords' cabin.

I went up to check on Matt again. He was quiet now, but how would he be when he awakened? I began to understand Bryce's anger toward the Beaches. Why wouldn't he resent having Matt grow up with people who clearly hated him and who would raise Matt to hate him too? They didn't care about Matt. All they cared about was their own vendetta with Bryce. Ed is right, I thought. These people are so involved with their own little world they can't see anything or anyone else.

It was midnight before the Larimers returned. They walked stiffly into the living room where I was waiting. "We're sorry to have kept you up so late, Anne," Mr. Larimer said, "but it couldn't be helped." His face, always pale, had a blanched look. "I think we made a mistake coming up here this summer," he said. "We thought . . ." But he didn't finish his sentence.

"We're taking Matt back to the city with us for the rest of the summer," Mrs. Larimer said. "It's by far the best solution. We'll be leaving the day after tomorrow. We'd go immediately but I need some time to close up the cabin. We're awfully sorry to have made such a botch of your summer, Anne, but we'll pay you for the whole season. It's the least we can do, and of course we'll look forward to your being Matt's sitter in the city; you've done wonders with him. I only wish we could explain . . ."

"No need for explanations," Mr. Larimer said hurriedly. "I'm sure Anne will take us at our word that we know what's best for Matt. Now I think it's time for all of us to get some sleep. And tomorrow with Matt, Anne, just act as though nothing has happened, but be sure to stay close to him. If for any reason you can't, call one of us. Otherwise, these next two days, let's try to make everything as normal as possible for him."

I wanted to tell the Larimers that Bryce was leaving Lakeville in a day or two, that there was no reason for them to go back to the city, but I couldn't say that without revealing that I'd met Bryce. I was trapped. And I was angry with the Larimers. Perhaps it was because they were so much in control of my life and Matt's. First my parents took away the things I had always depended on and now the Larimers were spoiling my whole summer with their paranoia. And what about Matt? Who were they to say he was never to see his own father?

In the morning Matt would have his tennis lesson at nine. I supposed he would not want to have the lesson, but I would talk him into it. While he was with the tennis pro, I would walk to Grass Lake and leave a message for Bryce. I wrote it out: DEAR BRYCE, THEY ARE TAKING MATT AWAY TOMORROW. IF YOU WANT TO SEE HIM, LEAVE A NOTE TELLING US WHERE WE CAN MEET YOU.

14

In the morning Matt was listless and groggy, hardly touching his breakfast. He had that distracted look I had noticed when I first took care of him. The other keepers all went out of their way to be nice to him, urging him to try the French toast and sausages, talking about how lucky he was to be getting away from the Beaches, how boring the summer was getting to be, and how August was always cold and rainy. Even Lance chimed in and tried to start a conversation with Matt about Matt's toad. Matt paid no attention to them. He just sat there waiting for breakfast to be over. When we went outside he said, "I'm not going to take any tennis lesson."

I was ready for that. "Listen, Matt, if you take your lesson, I'll let you see your father." Matt's expression changed immediately. "Be sure not to tell anyone," I warned him.

He looked at me with a sly expression that troubled me. "You think I'm crazy?" he said.

Matt's slyness gave me second thoughts. I remembered how back in Colonial Gardens Matt had confided in me. "Annie, if you promise not to tell, I'll let you in on a secret. I get so sick of my grandparents watching me that sometimes I wait up until I'm sure they're asleep. Then I get out of bed and get dressed and sneak down the stairs and turn off the alarm system. I go outside all by myself and walk up and down the streets with no one watching me. Sometimes for a whole hour." Horrified, I had made Matt promise me not to do that anymore.

In arranging a meeting between Matt and his father, wasn't I encouraging Matt to deceive his grandparents? Then remembering the sight of Matt the night before, lying in bed, drugged, I told myself the behavior of the Larimers was so bizarre, so irrational, that it called for extreme measures. I left the message.

After lunch Matt and I walked back to Grass Lake. When I checked the tree, there was a note from Bryce: ANNIE, YOU AND MATT MEET ME THIS AFTERNOON AT FOUR AT THE LANDING.

The Larimers were busy packing clothes and getting the cabin ready to close for the season. Mrs. Larimer said, "Don't go far from the cabin." Otherwise they left us alone.

It was easy to slip into the woods and walk to the landing, but I hated the deception. "I'm beginning to feel really sneaky," I told Matt.

"It's their fault for making us sneak around," Matt said.

We were at the landing a few minutes early. Matt's flashlight was where he had dropped it the night before in his struggle with his grandfather. Otherwise the landing looked as it always did when we came down to practice casting—peaceful, the river moving over the ridges of bottom sand and bright stones. I expected Bryce to materialize from somewhere in the woods. Instead, we saw a canoe round the bend of the river.

Bryce steered the canoe over to the bank and jumped out. "Come on," he said. "I want to show Matt a few paddling tricks."

Matt was climbing into the canoe. "Wait," I said. "What if someone should see us? I think we should go into the woods."

"No," Matt said. "Please, Annie, let's go for a ride. I want to see my dad go fast in the canoe."

Ever since I had decided to leave the note for Bryce I had felt a kind of recklessness. No matter what I did, everything would be ending. I would be leaving the Beaches and Ed and probably Matt, too. In spite of what the Larimers had promised, I guessed that once we were back in the city I would be an embarrassing reminder to them of what had happened over the summer. But I no longer cared about what the Larimers thought. I only cared about Matt and giving him some pleasure before he was dragged back to the city and away from his father. "All right," I said, "but we have to be back in half an hour at the latest."

There was a pleasant coolness rising from the stream. Maple trees bent across the narrow stretch of water, their green crowns nearly touching. Bryce was working at the paddling, which was upstream and difficult against the river's strong current. Matt sat up in the front of the canoe struggling to manipulate his large paddle. "Look, Matt," Bryce said, "why don't you just sit still and leave your paddle alone. We'll make better time."

Matt's feelings were hurt; he wanted to believe he was doing his part.

Bryce must have noticed, because he said, "You can paddle coming back. It's much easier downstream. It's hard for me to steer going upstream." Matt lay the paddle in the canoe.

"This is where Thomas taught me to fly-fish," Matt said, "and where you saw the bear, Annie." We were coming to the meadow.

"I know all about that," Bryce said.

"How do you know?" Matt asked.

"Because I saw Annie there."

"You didn't tell me, Annie." Matt was puzzled. There was too much he didn't know.

I tried to change the subject. "What's that pretty pinkish-red flower along the stream?"

"Loosestrife, and if you could see the damage it can do you wouldn't think it was so pretty." Bryce didn't want the subject changed. "I'll show you some fly-fishing tricks Thomas never heard of, Matt. Your granddad could catch ten trout for every one of Thomas's. You're finished hanging around Thomas."

"Why?" Matt asked. "I really like Thomas. He—"

"Just be quiet for a few minutes, will you, Matt?" interrupted Bryce. "This stretch of the river is full of deadheads. Keep your eyes open and your mouth shut."

We were past the meadow and coming into the cedar swamp. Matt was silenced but it wasn't a happy silence. I was quiet, too, wondering just what Bryce meant by promising Matt he would go fishing with him. The cedar swamp shut out the sunlight. Everything, even the water, was a dark, black green. "I think we ought to turn back," I said. "It's getting late."

"Not yet, Annie," Matt pleaded. "We'll be going downstream when we go back and I'll be helping then. It'll be a lot faster."

I didn't like Bryce's silence. "I suppose your father used to take you down the river when you were Matt's age," I said to him.

"Sure he took me down the stream. He knew it better than anyone. The Beaches think they own this property. The person who knows it best owns it, and they just tolerate someone else on it. If I wanted to, I could keep every last member of the Beaches off this land. I could pick them off from behind trees, or I could set the whole damn club on fire, but I don't have to do that. Nature is going to. The sand dunes are going to smother the club, and Lake Michigan is going to rise and wash over it. It's like that loosestrife you thought was so pretty. That weed grows so fast it can choke up whole rivers and kill them. They think they've got this perfect Eden, but they're evil and they're going to get kicked out just like they kicked my dad out."

The cold air from the swamp and Bryce's terrible words made me shiver. Matt was silent. He looked frightened. I couldn't let it go. "I don't know why you hate the club so much," I said. "Maybe they were hard on your father, but he had no business stealing from them. And what did they ever do to you?"

"I'll tell you what they did to me. They seduced Jess with their money and all the little things they kept giving her. They made her dissatisfied with everything she had. Her mother used to send her checks and Jess would go up to Blue Harbor and spend more on a rug or a dress than I would make in a whole month. I tried to keep her from going to the Beaches but she'd sneak over there. She was finished with me. She wanted to go back there for good and take Matt with her, and then Matt would belong to the Beaches. She didn't get away from me, and Matt won't either."

Matt had turned around in the canoe and was watching his father. At first he didn't know what to make of Bryce's outburst. I think he wanted to believe it was some sort of joke, but there was no mistaking Bryce's hatred.

"Why are you saying stuff like that about my grandparents?" he asked. Last night he had been furious with the Larimers because they were keeping him away from Bryce. Now he didn't know what to think.

We came out of the swamp and there were fields on either side of us. The surprise of the sun was amazing; it was as though we had never known anything but darkness. We began to see birds. First a scarlet tanager flew out of a hemlock, a red explosion against the green tree. Minutes later we saw yellow warblers darting in and out of the alder bushes at the stream's bank. Bryce drew his paddle out of the water, letting the canoe drift silently by the alders so the warblers would not be disturbed. Then we saw the indigo bunting. The tiny bird darted out from an overhanging branch. Matt and I had never seen one, and Bryce named it for us. The sun and the birds should have calmed my fears. Instead, what I saw made me panic. There was a road leading across the field to the riverbank, and parked on the road was a truck.

I knew exactly what Bryce was going to do. And I also knew there was no way I could stop him. I could only dumbly watch what was going to happen, and it happened almost immediately. Bryce maneuvered the canoe onto the bank. "You can get out here," he told Matt. "You, too, Annie."

"No," I said. "We have to go back."

Matt climbed out of the canoe. "What are we going to do? Why is the truck here?"

"I'm going to drive you back to the Beaches. Like Annie says: it's getting late." He reached over and, grabbing my arm, pulled me out of the canoe. "Help me put the canoe up on the truck, Matt." Matt couldn't pick the canoe up, but he dragged his end toward the truck. Bryce lifted the canoe up onto the truck bed.

"You get in, Matt." Obediently Matt started to climb into the pickup.

I knew it was hopeless, but I couldn't let Matt go without trying to stop Bryce. "Matt, don't get in that truck."

"Why not?" He still didn't understand.

"Bryce is going to take you with him."

"Where?"

Bryce got into the truck and, reaching across the seat, pulled Matt inside. He slammed the door. Through the closed window I saw Matt's lips move, but I couldn't hear him. I think he was saying my name. In a minute the truck had pulled away.

15

I knew I had to find my way to the Beaches as soon as possible. Catching Bryce before he got too far was the only hope there was for getting Matt back. I was afraid to risk the narrow trails that threaded through the woods, knowing I might take a wrong turn and get lost, for then Matt would be gone forever. I couldn't forget the look on Matt's face. He knew he had been betrayed by Bryce and by me, too, for hadn't I encouraged the deception? Complicity. The hateful word had a skipping sound, as if it were something cheerful.

I began to follow the river downstream. I ran through the meadow's tall grass, scaring up dragonflies and grasshoppers. The river was bright in the sun. There was nothing around me to suggest what had happened, so that for a few minutes I was almost able to believe it was some trick of my imagination. I saw myself arriving at the Beaches just in time to meet a perfectly safe Matt whom Bryce had dropped off. "He was just kidding, Annie," Matt would say.

But I had forgotten about the cedar swamp. It was when I reached the swamp and began climbing over the dead trees and falling into the holes of black water that I realized Matt was gone, maybe forever, and that it was my fault. Bryce had planned this all along, making his preparations, waiting until I gave him his chance. By now he would have abandoned the truck for a car he had hidden away.

It was only late afternoon but the sun was below the tops of the cedar trees. Darkness spilled like black water into the swamp, making it hard to see the submerged logs that tripped me again and again and the holes with their soft, murky mud that sucked at my feet. There was silence and any movement I saw was all absence—frogs and turtles slipping away into the pools, birds moving up into the high branches where they were invisible. Nothing was staying.

By the time I was through the swamp and could run again it was after six. The children and their keepers would be having their dinner at the lodge. I passed the landing and saw the sharp V in the sand where Bryce had beached the canoe, waiting for Matt and me to climb into it, knowing that once we were on the river we would be in his territory and that he could do with us what he liked. I kept to the trail, too exhausted now to run, and then, at last, I was back at the Beaches. I knew what I must do and I was terrified. I followed the trail to the Larimers' cabin. The Larimers were on the front porch with the Bradfords. They were all dressed for dinner. Their heads were bent toward one another and I had the feeling that even though no one was around they were speaking softly.

When I reached the porch they looked up. My clothes were splashed with water from my falls in the swamp, my face dirty where I had wiped away the sweat. I think they must have known immediately what had happened. Still Mrs. Larimer asked, "Where is Matt?"

On the way back, when I could think at all, I tried to make up a story that would absolve me—Bryce had just appeared out of nowhere and taken Matt. I had tried to fight with Bryce—I could point to the bruises from my falls. Instead, unexpectedly, helplessly, I told the truth; for which I give myself no credit. It was an impulse I couldn't control.

The Larimers didn't say a word. They were like people to whom so much had happened, the only thing they could imagine was another tragedy. Dr. Bradford swore. It was Mrs. Bradford who went to pieces. She turned on her husband and for a minute I thought she was going to strike him. "I told you," she said to him, her voice shaking. "I told you this would happen. You're all responsible. You should have gone to the police. You've let a murderer take Matt away."

"Margot, for God's sake," Dr. Bradford said. "Get hold

of yourself. This won't do anyone any good." He turned to me. "Give us a description of the truck."

I had memorized the license number. Mr. Larimer came to life. "I'll have to call the police." He went into the cabin. In a minute he was out again. "They're getting the description of the truck out. Thomas can go with us. He'll have an idea of what roads Bryce might take." He turned to Mrs. Larimer. "While we're gone, you tell Anne what happened. The police will want to question her and she's heard enough so that if she isn't briefed she might say the wrong thing. We'll tell the police she's too upset to be seen tonight and put them off until tomorrow." He put his arms around Mrs. Larimer. "We'll find Matt. I promise you."

"Can't I go?" I asked. I was desperate to do something. "I'd recognize the truck."

"We have the license number and we will certainly know Bryce," Dr. Bradford said. "Anyhow, by now he's probably ditched the truck somewhere. I don't think there's anything more you can do." His voice was cold.

The men left us. It was like all the old novels where the men go out to do vengeance and the women wait at home, helpless. I hated it. I didn't want to sit there and face what I had done. "Anne," Mrs. Larimer said, "don't blame yourself. We knew how dangerous Bryce was. It was unfair to give you a responsibility like that." She was like someone at a funeral trying to give polite comfort.

"You never should have protected Bryce," Mrs.

Bradford said. "If he were in jail like he should have been, this wouldn't have happened."

"In jail for what?" I asked. "Has Bryce tried to take Matt away before?" I couldn't let myself use the word "kidnap," with its frightening images of parents glued next to the telephone or agents breaking into an empty apartment, curtains blowing in the breeze of an open window.

"It's worse than that, Anne," Mrs. Larimer said. "But you have to swear never to repeat what you are going to hear. I've told you not to feel guilty about what happened, but you must recognize it was very poor judgment on your part, after all I said, to let Bryce see Matt behind our backs. If you had told us about that first meeting between Bryce and Matt, we could have returned to the city immediately. I'm not saying this to blame you, only to let you know you owe us something and that something is never to repeat what I am going to tell you."

I nodded my head, but I didn't want to hear any more. I suspected that what she would tell me was going to make me even more miserable. I longed to get into a car and drive up and down roads looking for Matt.

"I told you Jess was upset when she came here to the Beaches with Matt the night she had the accident. It was more than that. There had been a bad argument with Bryce. We guessed it was one of many. Jess had been miserable because Bryce had forbidden her to visit us or let us see Matt. He was still furious with the club for firing his father, even though we had a great deal of irrefutable evidence that his father was part of a poaching ring selling game from our property to restaurants downstate. When his father died of a heart attack, Bryce blamed us. And then he resented our giving Jess money. Perhaps we shouldn't have done that, but we hated to see her do without, and she was used to nice things.

"Of course Jess came to see us anyhow, but she didn't dare bring Matt. She was afraid Matt would say something about the Beaches in front of Bryce—and Bryce had a terrible temper. Jess never admitted it to us, but we suspect that Bryce had actually abused her." Mrs. Larimer's voice broke and she stopped for a minute and then went on as if she were under some horrible compulsion to tell the whole story and get it over with as quickly as possible. "The summers went by," she said, "with Matt just a few miles from us but with no chance to be with him. Sometimes Jess would call us to say Bryce was away and that she would have Matt play in their yard. Then we would drive by their house slowly, but not so slowly that Matt would realize who we were. Those were the only glimpses we had of our grandson. Last year on Labor Day weekend Jess had begged Bryce to let her take Matt to the Beaches, just the one time, before we left for the season. He refused. They had an argument and she put Matt in the car and came here. She said she would leave Matt with us and then go back and get her own things. She was through with Bryce.

"We didn't want her to return home, but she insisted

she owed it to Bryce to tell him that she and Matt were going back to the city with us. As soon as she left we began to worry. Mr. Larimer decided to follow her. He asked my brother, Dr. Bradford, and Thomas to go along in the event there was trouble. When they got to the farmhouse they found Jess dead and Bryce hysterical. It was a head wound. Bryce said he had struck her, knocking her against the edge of the table." When Mrs. Larimer saw the look on my face, she reached over and put her hand on mine. "Anne, I hate having to tell you this, but you have to understand what's at stake, how important it is that we get our stories straight. The only reason I can bear to say all of this out loud is that I've gone over it so many thousands of times in my own mind, trying to understand it.

"My brother and Mr. Larimer told Bryce that he was a murderer and would certainly be sent to jail. In exchange for promising never to see Matt again and for staying away from Lakeville, they said they would fix things so it would look like an accident. Dr. Bradford told my husband to remain in the farmhouse to keep an eye on Bryce. Then Dr. Bradford and Thomas put Jess in her own car and Dr. Bradford drove it to that dangerous curve on the way from Lakeville to the Beaches. Thomas followed them." Mrs. Larimer looked like she couldn't go on, but she did. "They put Jess in the driver's seat and sent the car crashing into the tree. I'll never know how my brother had the courage to do that. They went back for Mr. Larimer. By then Bryce had

117

calmed down and realized what it would mean if he were charged with murder. He swore he would agree to their conditions.

"The men were back at the Beaches for an hour before Thomas was sent to report to the police that he was driving home and found the car. The police arrived to notify us of the accident. When the police questioned us about Matt, we simply said he had been spending the day with us. It never occurred to them to think it unusual for Matt to be with his grandparents. They never questioned Matt. We told them he was too upset, and of course they were sympathetic. Matt thinks his mother died in an automobile accident.

"You must understand, we didn't do this for Bryce. Nothing would have pleased us more than to have Bryce put away for life. A day doesn't go by when I don't wish he were behind bars, and there are days when I want him dead. He killed our daughter. What we did, we did for Matt. What would Matt's life be if he and all the world knew his father was a murderer who was spending his life in jail for killing Matt's mother? You know what the media are like. They've always been fascinated by wealthy people. You can imagine how they would hound us, how they would follow Matt around. The trial would be front-page news for days. Each year on the anniversary of the murder everything would be raked up all over again. Reporters would swarm around the Beaches. All of Matt's friends would know. He'd be marked for the rest of his life—any school he went to, any job he took. Even if we gave up our home and Mr. Larimer gave up his position and we tried to hide somewhere with Matt, they would still hunt us down." Her voice was resolved, determined. Long ago she had decided what had been done was best for Matt and nothing would change her mind. It was what she said next that truly shocked me.

"Of course," she said, "we couldn't do it alone. Our friends at the Beaches had seen Jess come here with Matt, had seen how upset she was. They watched as Mr. Larimer and Dr. Bradford and Thomas rushed after Jess, and they saw the men return home. There was a meeting of the Beaches and we told everyone what had happened. You must have noticed how close we all are to one another. We've all grown up together and our parents and grandparents before us. There is very little we don't know about one another and nothing we wouldn't do for one another. Everyone at the meeting agreed with us . . ."

"I didn't," Mrs. Bradford said.

"No, that's true. Margot didn't," said Mrs. Larimer. "But everyone else did. They've all been wonderful, so understanding to us and so kind to Matt. Of course questions were raised. Lyle and Mabel and one of the maintenance men were a bit suspicious. That's why I tried to prepare you for rumors before we came here this summer, Anne. Thomas is the only one outside of the club members who knows what happened, but Thomas dislikes Bryce as much as we do. When the business with Bryce's father came up, Bryce tried to blame Thomas. Thomas has never said a word to anyone, nor has he ever asked for any privilege because of what he knows. He's very independent; he doesn't care what anyone thinks of him. We respect him for that and we trust him completely. I don't believe he approves of what we've done, but he would never make rules for someone else." She glanced at Margot Bradford for a moment.

"I know you think you did it for Matt," Margot Bradford said, "but deceptions are always dangerous. There's no foothold. It's all stumbling with nothing you can hang on to. It's not too late. We could still tell the truth and then the police would know what they're dealing with."

Mrs. Larimer was too upset to be patient. "Margot, use your head! If we told the police now, we would be accessories to our own daughter's murder. Think what the papers would do with that. Would you want to see your husband in jail?"

Then we three women waited in the darkening house for the men to return. I longed to leave them, to go up to my room, yet I knew I couldn't stand being alone. If Matt was gone forever, it would be my fault. I was trying to understand what the Larimers had done. I supposed that both Mr. Larimer and Dr. Bradford were used to making quick decisions that influenced the lives of others; in their professions it was a necessity. At the time I don't believe the word "arrogance" occurred to me because I had seen how much the Larimers loved Matt. Instead I thought of the courage, of the strength it must have taken them, to carry out their plan. But afterward, hadn't there been second thoughts, questions, doubts? Mrs. Larimer had said there had been a meeting at the Beaches, that all the members except Mrs. Bradford had agreed they had done the right thing. Or had they just agreed to support them whether they had done the right thing or not? My first thought was that it was good to have someone who would stand behind you no matter what you did, but then I wasn't sure. What if you had done wrong? Wasn't it up to your friends to tell you that?

The house had grown dark, but none of us thought to get up and turn on the lights. For different reasons we preferred the dark. When at last Mr. Larimer and Dr. Bradford walked into the cabin and snapped the light switch, the change was so abrupt we were too startled for a moment to ask what had happened. Mrs. Larimer got up as though whatever the news, she would face it standing. "The truck was found abandoned outside of Lakeville," Mr. Larimer said. "Bryce must have had another car hidden. I suppose he bought it under an assumed name or he might even have stolen it. They're checking the truck out. I've sent word round that there is to be a meeting tonight."

"It's almost midnight," Mrs. Larimer said.

"We can't waste a minute," Dr. Bradford told her. "Margot, dear, if you like, you can stay home."

"I'm coming," she said. Her husband looked at the Larimers and shrugged.

"You've told Anne everything?" Mr. Larimer asked his wife.

She nodded.

"Then I think it's best she come and talk to the club herself. We're all so upset, there may be questions that haven't occurred to us that someone else will think to ask her. Thomas is coming too."

16

The meeting took place in the Larimers' living room. For once Mrs. Larimer did not bother to plump the pillows or rearrange the flowers. She sat perfectly still, hardly responding to the embraces of the other members as they came into the house. The members had put on whatever clothes were handy. Instead of the perfectly turned out, sophisticated group I was used to, I saw the women without makeup and the men in wrinkled slacks and slippers. Judge Clements and his wife were the first to arrive, but there was no eagerness in their early appearance, only a kind of insistence on getting things over with. They might have been entering a dentist's office. As soon as Mrs. Thompson arrived she began pushing chairs around and, like an usher in a church, indicated where people ought to sit, until her husband rather forcefully took her arm and guided her to a seat. The Beamishes and Stocktons came together. The Parkers and the Brightmans and the Duncans were there. Before she sat down, Mrs. Duncan went over to Mrs. Larimer and hugged her, as all the women had, but then she came over and embraced me. "We all feel for you, Anne," she said. Mr. Peterson was talking in a low voice to Dr. Bradford and Mrs. Larimer; there seemed to be some point they disagreed on. Mr. Peterson shrugged and walked away and was already standing in front of the room, ready to begin, when the McKeans and Robertses finally arrived.

Mr. Peterson, the club president, called the meeting to order. I was surprised by the formality and even more surprised when the entire group, including the Larimers, rose and placed their hands over their hearts. For a moment I thought they were going to give the Pledge of Allegiance and looked around for a flag. But what happened was even more bizarre. In unison they recited: "We promise to uphold the traditions and values of Hawkins Bradford, to love his land and to be true to it, and to pass it on to our children, as it has been passed on to us."

Then they sat down. Mr. Peterson began with a polite little speech. "I want to say at once how much our hearts go out to Grace and Tucker Larimer at this difficult time. I'm sure I speak for all of us when I say that there is nothing we will not do to insure Matt's safe return. Now, the hour is late, so let us move right along. You have all come to know Anne, who has been Matt's keeper." (His use of the past tense did not escape me.)

He went on. "She is just as upset as we are over what has happened. Of course, she had no idea how dangerous it was to allow Bryce to get his hands on Matt. She is deeply sorry for what has occurred and has kindly volunteered to describe just what happened." He nodded at me.

For a moment I doubted if I could say one word, much less repeat the whole terrible, humiliating story of my deception. But what I sensed in the room was not hostility for the disaster I had caused but a supportive, encouraging feeling. It was as though I were surrounded by an all-forgiving family who wanted only to make things as easy as possible for me. Once I started, everyone listened sympathetically. Two or three times I was gently interrupted and a question or two asked of me, or I was encouraged to elaborate on some point.

When I finished Mr. Peterson thanked me and asked that Thomas be invited to come in, but before he was summoned Mrs. Bradford got up. "I want to make it clear to Anne that none of this is her fault."

Dr. Bradford tried to make her sit down. "No one is suggesting that, Margot. Pete was very clear on that."

But she ignored him. "All of you know I was against keeping Jess's murder a secret from the police." At the mention of the word "murder" a little murmur of disapproval went through the group. "There's no point in denying it. We all know it was murder. You see what it has led to. We've set ourselves up as gods with our own justice and our own laws. And now you want to do it all over again. Why are we meeting here? Why don't we just let the police take over?"

Mr. Larimer was on his feet. "Margot, dear, no one wants Matt back more than I do, but the police don't understand the urgency for the simple reason that you yourself stated. They don't know Jess's death was . . ." He couldn't say the word. "They don't understand what Bryce is capable of. They don't know how important it is that Matt be found immediately. It has to be done by someone who understands all of the ramifications of what has happened. And we are the only ones who do."

In spite of what I had been told, in spite of what had been said that evening, it wasn't until I heard the words "what Bryce is capable of" that I realized what everyone was thinking. It wasn't just that Bryce had taken Matt. If Bryce had killed Jess to keep her from returning to the Beaches, he might kill Matt for the same reason. I thought of the orchids scattered on the steps of the lodge. It hadn't mattered that the orchids meant a great deal to Bryce, that he would have done anything to protect them. At the moment he destroyed them, all that mattered to him was that he was getting back at the Beaches, that he was taking the orchids away from the Beaches forever. I had merely despised myself for my stupidity. Now I saw myself for what I was: a possible accomplice to a murder. I was paralyzed with fright and guilt. I hardly noticed Dr. Bradford taking his wife out of the meeting. There was more conversation, but I didn't hear it. Minutes went by before I could pull myself together enough to notice what was going on. By then Thomas was in the room and, after his fashion, answering questions.

"Yes," he was saying, "I knew his daddy well as anyone did. He and I worked here together for twenty-three years till you kicked him out. I don't blame you for that. He was stealing right under your noses, but you could have had a talk with him. If it comes to taking things that don't belong to you, you can ask yourselves who this land belonged to in the first place."

No one seemed surprised at these remarks. Evidently Thomas had said similar things before. Everyone appeared to take his charges with a grain of salt. "Yes," he said, answering a question Mr. Peterson put to him, "I got an idea where Bryce might be."

There was absolute silence. Everyone was alert. "Why the hell didn't you say so before?" Mr. Larimer said, looking like he wanted to choke the words out of Thomas.

Thomas shrugged. "It just came to me when I started talking about Bryce's daddy." I'm not sure they believed him, but I had seen him with Matt and I knew he would do his best to get Matt back—not for the club's sake but for Matt's.

"Please tell us, Thomas." Mr. Peterson was making a show of patience.

"Bryce's daddy had an old hunting shack in the Upper Peninsula near Newberry. It wasn't anything but a lean-to to keep you warm and a place to put a cot and a few groceries. We had some good times up there." You could imagine the slovenly cabin, the bottle on the table, the unshaven men topping one another's stories.

"Can you give us directions?" Mr. Larimer asked.

"I could go up there with you," Thomas suggested.

"No. We'll go alone," Dr. Bradford said.

Thomas seemed to understand. "I can tell you how to get there, all right."

Some of the other members had questions. "At this point shouldn't we call in the police?" Mr. Duncan said.

"That's impossible," Mr. Larimer said. "The police know only what we choose to tell them. What they don't know is just how deadly Bryce can be. And if they don't know that, they're apt to march right into his cabin, giving him plenty of warning to do whatever he wants to." Mr. Larimer's voice was steady, as if he were discussing a situation that hardly involved him. Although they were all close, even intimate friends, the structure was that of a meeting, of business set forth and accomplished, a formality that kept everyone, especially the Larimers, from giving way to panic.

"I'd be happy to go with you," Mr. Peterson said, and immediately the other men volunteered.

Dr. Bradford thanked them. "We appreciate your offers, but I think a small party will be the most effective."

Then, almost as an aside, Mr. Stockton said, "I don't

128

suppose any of us would want Matt to go through his childhood terrified of being kidnapped again."

Mrs. Peterson, who was wearing a robe and slippers, said in a very firm voice, "Matt has been made to suffer enough." And to Mr. and Mrs. Larimer she added, "So have Grace and Tucker. We have to end this once and for all. Of course, I can speak only for myself, but I suspect you have the support of everyone here." There were general sounds of agreement. Only the Duncans were quiet.

Listening to them, I thought they misunderstood Bryce. They seemed to suggest that Dr. Bradford and Mr. Larimer could talk some sense into Bryce, to convince him to stop troubling them. Looking back, I am appalled at my innocence. I see now that because I said nothing the others assumed I agreed with them, and so I became one of them, accepted at last not because of my loyalty but because of my stupidity.

The rest of the meeting was brief. Dr. Bradford and Mr. Larimer were to leave at once. If anyone, especially the police, questioned their departure, they were to be told that the two men had returned to the city. Since the next day was Monday, and they usually went back at the end of the weekend, it was unlikely that questions would be asked. Family arguments over a child's custody were not that unusual. The police probably handled several in the course of the year.

The Petersons were asked to rehearse with me the story I would tell the police. They urged me to get a good night's sleep and "suggested" I meet with them immediately after breakfast. "No need to eat with the keepers and the children; they'll have too many questions. Have your breakfast with us." I didn't know whether their suggestion was a kindness to spare me the questions or whether it was a precaution because they were afraid I might give something away.

After the meeting, while everyone said good night to the Larimers, Thomas came over to me on his way out of the cabin. "You should leave tomorrow and go back home," he said quietly. Then he left me. At first I thought of his remark as a threat, but later I saw he was doing me a kindness.

17

The sheriff and one of his deputies, clearly impressed and a little nervous to be at the Beaches, arrived early the next morning to talk with me. Respectful, almost deferential, they cast surreptitious looks around the Larimers' cabin, taking it all in. Then you could see them recalling their reason for being there. The Petersons explained to the sheriff that Mrs. Larimer was too "distressed" to see them but that I would be glad to answer any questions they might have. "We needn't tell you," Mr. Peterson said to them, "that Anne is very upset, too, so we'd appreciate your keeping the interview as brief as possible."

"Yes, sir." The sheriff seemed eager to show his command of the situation. Turning to me, he said, "If you'll tell us in your own words just what happened, I'll save any questions for later." He looked at the deputy, who, recognizing the cue, took out a notebook and a pencil.

"Matt and I were at the landing."

Mr. Peterson interrupted me. "You know where the landing is, Sheriff?"

"Oh, yes," the sheriff said, and then added, "Well, just about." Perhaps on second thought the sheriff had decided he ought not to appear too familiar with the landing's location. Ed had told me that early in the spring, before the club members arrived at the Beaches, the local residents of Lakeville used the road across from the landing to get into the stream to fish along the Beaches' property.

"Matt and I used to go there nearly every afternoon," I said, "so Matt could practice his fly casting. Well, yesterday he was wading in the stream and there was a truck parked on the road across from the landing. I didn't recognize the man inside. I had never seen Matt's father, but Matt knew who it was right away. The man got out of the truck and called Matt over to him. Matt climbed out of the stream and walked to the truck. I still didn't know who it was or I would have called Matt back. The man told Matt to get into the truck and sort of pushed Matt when Matt hesitated. By then I realized something very wrong was happening, so I started calling to Matt to come back, but the man had climbed into the truck and locked the doors. Before I could do anything, the truck was gone. I ran right back to the Larimers to tell them."

"That's when we called you, Sheriff," Mr. Peterson said.

"Did Matt see his father regular?" the sheriff asked.

"No," Mr. Peterson said. "Bryce went away after his wife's death. He was very depressed. The Larimers took care of Matt."

"Well, when Bryce came back, didn't he make any move to see Matt? He was in the canoe race, so he must have been around a couple of days. We heard other people had seen him in town."

"To tell you the truth, Sheriff, Bryce hadn't shown much interest in Matt. Of course, had he come to the Larimers and asked to see Matt, there would have been no problem. You've probably heard the rumors that Bryce didn't get along too well with us here. I'm sure there was fault on both sides. There was that business with his father, which he blamed on us when actually we put up with that man's poaching for years. The truth is, Bryce had a grudge against the club."

The deputy, a young man who had been sitting rigidly on the edge of a chair taking notes, now asked, "Just who had legal custody of the boy?"

The sheriff must have thought the question too abrupt, because he softened it by adding, "I suppose some arrangements must have been made when the Larimers' daughter died."

"Oh, yes," Mr. Peterson said. "The judge down in

the city gave custody to the Larimers. Bryce had agreed to that. He didn't know what his plans would be." The last sentence was addressed to the deputy with a smile that was aimed toward the sheriff, as though Mr. Peterson and the sheriff, together, were humoring the deputy. "Well," Mr. Peterson said, "if that's all . . ."

The sheriff thanked the Petersons, nodded at me, and then, pushing the deputy ahead of him, bowed himself out of the room like a courtier in a Shakespearean play.

The Petersons told me how well I had done. "We don't like having to ask that you stretch the truth a little, Anne, but you understand we're just doing what is best for Matt. I'm sure that's what you want too."

Later, when Meredith asked where Matt was, I hesitated, not knowing what to say, but Syrie was ready for the question. "He's visiting his dad, not that it's any of your business." The other children seemed to accept the answer.

I spent the rest of the morning at Grass Lake trying to stay out of everyone's way. A duck with her string of ducklings swam along the far edge of the lake. A blue heron high-stepped its way around the shore looking for frogs and crayfish. I noticed a ripple in the water and saw a lithe brown body undulating on the lake's surface. In a moment it had disappeared beneath the water. At first I thought it was a beaver, but that would be unusual in the middle of the day. After a few minutes of watching, I decided it was an otter, and in spite of my misery, I was excited. Otters were rare, even at the

Beaches, where so much of the land was wild. At first I believed the otter was something good sent as a sign I was forgiven. I changed my mind as I watched it slink around in the water, diving and swimming in circles, then disappearing until it was inches from the string of ducklings. The mother duck hit the water with her wings, signaling danger, directing the ducklings to follow her. I found myself screeching at the otter. Whether it was from the action of the duck or my shouts, the otter dived beneath the water's surface and disappeared.

In the afternoon I went back to Grass Lake. The first thing I did was count the ducklings. They were all there. But the otter was so graceful, its fur so sleek and its face so sweet, that although I knew what might happen to the ducklings, I was disappointed when the afternoon went by and the otter didn't return.

That evening there was a phone call from Mr. Larimer. I was in the room when it came, or I'm not sure Mrs. Larimer would have told me what her husband said. Our conversation all day had consisted of polite banalities. "Bryce and Matt are there" was all she said. I wanted to ask "What will happen now?" but her manner didn't invite questions. I heard her walking downstairs around two in the morning. When I came down at five she was up and dressed. "I've made coffee and toast," she said. "I won't be going over to the lodge for breakfast."

"I'll stay with you." I knew she wouldn't leave the phone.

"I wanted this to be a happy summer for you, Anne. I've never mentioned it because I didn't think you would want me to, but I've known about your parents' divorce, and I had hoped this would be a chance for you to forget all of that. Instead we seem to have made things worse for you."

By the end of the day there was no longer any attempt at polite conversation. The silence between us was not an angry one. Mrs. Larimer did not blame me for what had happened to Matt. It was just that she was thinking only of her husband and brother's mission. She sat quietly in a chair, her face pale, her hands folded in her lap. Had she been a religious person, she would surely have had a prayer book open or a rosary twined in her hands.

I tried to imagine what would happen when the men confronted Bryce. I supposed they were waiting for Bryce to leave Matt, perhaps to go into a town for supplies. Then they would free Matt and bring him back to the Beaches. But that would be just the beginning. Bryce would try to get Matt back. The threat of Bryce would remain, more dangerous than ever.

Of one thing I was sure. As soon as Matt returned to the Beaches, and the police had no further need of me, I would be sent home. I would certainly never be trusted with Matt again.

The women spent more time together that day and the next than usual. There were no golf games or trips into Blue Harbor. Even the tennis courts were deserted.

They gathered on porches doing their needlepoint or just drinking iced tea and looking out at the lake. The evening of the second day another call came. This time I wasn't in the room, but I had just come into the upstairs hallway. I could hear Mrs. Larimer, but I don't think she knew I was there.

"Is he all right?" I heard her ask. And then, "Thank God," so perhaps she had prayed after all. "And . . ." She seemed to be searching for a way to put her question. "And everything else is taken care of?" She was asking when they would be home when I went quietly into my room, waited a minute or two, and then came noisily into the hall and down the stairway.

"Did I hear the phone ring?" I asked.

"Wonderful news, Anne. They're bringing Matt home."

I was afraid to ask about Bryce, but Mrs. Larimer understood what I wanted to say. "There's no need to worry about Bryce," she said.

18

Matt's return the next afternoon was not what I expected. I had imagined the joyful scenes and tearful embraces of storybooks. Instead Mrs. Larimer greeted her husband and grandson with reserve. Of course there were hugs and a suggestion of tears, hastily wiped away, and long, hungry surreptitious looks at Matt, but no one allowed their real feelings to show. Even Matt appeared impassive, almost wooden. I sensed that Matt's indifference was a kind of numbness. I worried about what would happen to him when the shock wore off. He sat down a little way off from us, as though he deliberately chose not to join us.

Mrs. Bradford came over and the six of us gathered

in the large living room while Mrs. Larimer passed around lemonade and iced tea as though nothing had happened, as if Matt and the two men had just returned from some excursion. The questions when they came were startling for what they did not ask. There were questions on how the drive down from the Upper Peninsula went—very little traffic; some remarks to Matt on what had happened at the Beaches in the two days Matt had been gone—Meredith had won the sailboard race, a first for a girl at the Beaches; and a discussion of how soon the men would be returning to the city—immediately. There were no questions about what had happened to Matt, how they had found him, or where Bryce was.

Only Mrs. Bradford dwelled on what had happened. "Are you all right?" she kept asking Matt, to which he nodded, looking as if he wished she would let him alone. Instead of seeming pleased with what her husband and Mr. Larimer had accomplished, Mrs. Bradford appeared to be hostile toward them, refusing to look their way or to acknowledge anything they said to her. Finally she said, "This is the end of the Beaches."

For a moment there was silence and then Dr. Bradford said, "Margot, it's all over with now. We have Matt back safe and sound."

"Nothing is safe and certainly nothing is sound," was her curious answer. After that she said little.

If Mrs. Bradford's behavior was odd, Matt's behavior was alarming in its quietness. He had nothing to say.

He might have been in another room for all the attention he paid to us. He poked at the ice cubes in his glass and stared at the floor. When questions were addressed to him, he merely nodded or shook his head. He refused to look at me.

By late afternoon everyone at the Beaches knew Matt was back but with polite restraint no one came to intrude. That seemed unnatural to me. I would have expected a roomful of excited friends. It was what the occasion called for. Instead the Bradfords returned home and Mr. Larimer went upstairs to change into his business suit. Mrs. Larimer started to go with him, leaving me with Matt. Halfway up the stairs she turned. "Anne, you and Matt do whatever you like this afternoon," she said. "You can stay inside and rest if that's what Matt feels like, or you might like to go out for a little walk and Matt can stretch his legs after the long ride."

I had been sure that I would be sent home. Sent home in disgrace was the way I thought of it. I knew it was what I deserved. I was surprised by Mrs. Larimer's suggestion. I thought I would be the last person in the world they would leave Matt with. I had betrayed their confidence and made it possible for Bryce to kidnap Matt. I couldn't help asking of Mrs. Larimer, "Now that Matt's back, when should I plan on going home?"

"You aren't going to leave us, Anne?" Her voice was full of surprise and hurt, but the effect was somehow less than natural. I felt she had anticipated my question and rehearsed the answer.

Uncertainly I said, "After everything, I didn't think you would want me to stay."

"There was never any question of your leaving, Anne. You're one of us. And now more than ever Matt needs stability in his life. Get out in the sunshine—you'll feel much better for some exercise."

I guessed she wanted the cabin for herself and Mr. Larimer so that all the questions she hadn't asked in front of me and Matt she could ask now.

I saw that for Matt's sake things were to appear as ordinary and normal as possible, but I was sure from the way Matt acted that he didn't think everything was ordinary and normal. The pretending seemed foolish, not only foolish but harmful to Matt, as though what he had gone through, what all of us had gone through, didn't really matter. Matt was thinking about it, I was thinking about it, the Larimers were thinking about it. Why couldn't we talk about it? Something else bothered me, but I couldn't quite decide what it was.

"Where will we go?" I asked Matt when we were outside. A couple of the keepers and their charges were on the beach. When they saw us they waved, and Syrie applauded when she saw Matt, but no one approached us.

"I don't care," Matt said.

We wandered along the boardwalk until we were out of sight of the others. I dropped onto the sand, welcoming its warmth, and Matt settled down beside me and stared out at the lake. Club members seldom came that far to swim; the lake bottom there was rocky and Thomas didn't groom that section of the beach. The encroaching sand from the dunes had formed small hills over which wild grapevines trailed. The green leaves looked fresh and cool against the hot sand.

Matt was as I remembered him when I first started working for the Larimers in Colonial Gardens. In just a few days his tan had grown sallow. He looked thin and I saw he was biting his nails again. I felt I had to find a way to break through his sullen reserve, to get back on our old footing. I thought he might be blaming me for what had happened. "Matt," I said, "I'm sorry about everything. I never should have let you see Bryce."

"It's not your fault. I wanted to see him. If you hadn't let me, I probably would have sneaked away. That's how dumb I was about my dad."

"Was it very bad?"

"Not at first. It was sort of fun. My dad had food stashed away in the trunk of the car we changed to. He had clothes for us and fishing rods and everything. He had planned it all out. After we got in the car we just kept driving. I wasn't really worried then because I thought he'd only keep me for a week or two so we could go fishing or hunting or something. And anyhow, I'd been with my grandmother and grandfather for a long time, so I thought it should be his turn, and he was really nice to me on the way to the Upper Peninsula.

"But when we got to the shack he was different. He wouldn't let me go outdoors. He had some maps of

Canada he showed me, and he said that in a day or two, when he had everything together, that's where we'd go. I asked him when I was going back to the Beaches and he said never . . . that the Beaches was an evil place. I mean, he really hated everyone here." The corner of Matt's mouth was twitching.

"You don't have to tell me if you don't want to."

"I can't tell anyone else. My grandparents don't want to hear. They said I should forget everything. The worst thing was at night. He'd chain my leg to the cot so I couldn't get away while he slept. It wasn't tight or anything, but when he did it I knew he was crazy. And he had a gun. Not the kind for hunting but one for shooting people. He slept with it under his pillow. He said he'd use it on anyone who tried to take me back to the Beaches. He even said he'd use it on me and him if someone tried to take me back."

I hadn't known Bryce at all.

"How did your grandfather and Dr. Bradford get you away?"

"Last night . . ." Matt paused, and I could see that he was thinking how impossible it was that it had only been one night ago. "Last night just after dark my dad was looking out the window of the shack and he said, 'There must be a grass fire.' He called me to the window. The fire was quite a way away, but it was getting closer and Dad was worried. He ran out to see what was happening and Granddad and Uncle Don were waiting just outside the door."

"What did they do?"

"They had hold of my dad and they were tying him up. He looked like he was unconscious. They told me to stay inside and I could tell from the way they said it they really meant it. I watched from the window though. They went and got their car. When they got back they put my dad in his car and my granddad drove the car. Uncle Don was following them in his car.

"After a while Granddad and Uncle Don came back and they said they had had a long talk with my dad and he promised to go far away and never bother us again."

Matt was too nervous to sit still, so we began walking along the shore, beachcombing in the old way we used to, picking up gull feathers, shells, bits of odd-shaped driftwood, and wet stones that looked interesting but which would soon dry to a dull color. Matt found a thin oval stone and flung it out into the lake. It arced again and again over the water. "My dad would have been surprised at how many times that skipped," Matt said.

I was shocked to hear Matt speak of his father without bitterness, but what was even more disturbing was his use of the past tense in referring to Bryce. Finally I understood what had been bothering me. Mrs. Larimer had told Matt and me to go outside and get some exercise. She had not said, "Stay close to the cabin." Perhaps she felt after what had happened it was not necessary to warn me, that the danger of Bryce reappearing would certainly be on my mind.

But Dr. Bradford and Mr. Larimer had gone back to the city. Why weren't they staying at the Beaches to be sure Bryce didn't return? And why hadn't the police been notified to watch out for Bryce? Why hadn't someone been hired to help Lyle patrol the Beaches? Why were they so confident? They might have given Bryce a great deal of money or threatened him with kidnapping charges, but Matt's description of Bryce certainly showed he was not rational, that none of those things would stop him from trying to get Matt away from the Beaches. In another setting the answer might be obvious, but here it seemed impossible, and I put it out of my mind.

Matt and I stood at the edge of the large lake. It was one of those early August days when the first chill suggests autumn and makes summer more precious. The lake was still and the voices of the children in the distance and the shrill call of the gulls were the only sounds. I couldn't imagine a more peaceful place. I didn't allow myself to think about where Bryce was. I put him out of my mind. I was relieved that they were letting me stay at the Beaches. If the Larimers were not worried, I would not be either. After a while Matt and I wandered back to the cabin. The sheriff was in the living room.

"Well, so here's the missing boy," he said when he saw Matt. He had taken his cue from Mrs. Larimer and was trying to be offhand.

"Yes, and he's just fine. You didn't have to come all the way over here, Sheriff. We just called you to let you know that everything was all right and the agreement with Matt's father perfectly amicable."

"Well, that may be and I'm certainly glad, but the fact is, he did break the law. It's a lucky thing he didn't take the boy over the state line or up to Canada. If he had, the FBI would have to be called in."

"There's absolutely no need to think about something like that. We look at it as a little family misunderstanding. Bryce is on his way out west, and prosecuting him and having Matt testify and all the publicity that would go with it is the last thing in the world we want. It wouldn't be good for Matt."

The sheriff examined Matt, who certainly looked miserable enough. "Well . . ."

"Thanks so much, Sheriff," Mrs. Larimer said, "and don't forget to talk to Thomas this fall. Before he went back to the city, Mr. Larimer mentioned to Thomas that you and the deputy might want to do a little hunting at the Beaches. The club knows it's better to keep the herd of deer culled."

"I don't know about the deputy, but I'd sure appreciate a chance to do a little hunting here." The sheriff walked over to Matt and ruffled his hair in a good-natured way. Matt smiled up at him. The sheriff didn't know Matt well enough to understand how false the smile was.

19

As the week went on Matt and I settled into the security of routine. Matt went back to his tennis and sailing lessons. The other children treated Matt with a certain amount of deference. They knew he had been through some dangerous adventure and they longed to ask him for details, but their parents and keepers had warned them against mentioning anything about Matt's absence. Before, he had been the odd child out. Now their attitude was one of fascination. They jostled one another for the chance to sit next to him and chose him for games. In their uneventful lives at the Beaches he had become the one interesting thing, the one exotic, but none of this was ever mentioned in front of us. If they talked about it among themselves, they were properly silent in front of Matt and me.

One disturbing thing happened. Mrs. Bradford packed up and left the day after Matt got back. I saw her on the steps of her cabin, dressed in city clothes, which looked odd in the rustic setting. When I looked more closely at her linen suit, I noticed the buttons on her blouse were not all done up and the blouse itself was half pulled out of her skirt. Thomas was helping her with suitcases and boxes. "Anne, come and say good-bye to me," she called. It would have been rude to ignore her, but for some reason I didn't want to talk to her. She saw me hesitate. "Just for a minute."

I walked over. "If you hurry you could get your things together. I'll wait and you can go back with me." I must have looked surprised, because she said, "I know it's sudden, but you must feel that things are not right here. If you don't leave now you won't ever leave."

I couldn't imagine what she meant. "I'll be going back at the end of the summer," I said. I saw the strain on her face and the nervous way she kept clenching and unclenching her hands.

"You'll be going back physically," she said, "but if you don't leave now, you'll be a part of the Beaches for the rest of your life." I must have looked pleased at the prospect, because she turned and walked back into her cabin, closing the door behind her and leaving me alone. Thomas watched me come down the porch stairs.

"What happened to Bryce?" I asked him.

He turned away without answering me.

Suddenly I felt afraid and began to run back to the cabin with some idea of getting my things, perhaps confronting Mrs. Larimer and then leaving with Margot Bradford. Mrs. Larimer was sitting on the porch and I realized she had seen everything that had happened at the Bradfords' cabin. She sat quietly, her hands working a needlepoint pillow, pink and mauve roses against a pale-green background. The white wicker furniture shone in the bright sunlight. The reflection of the sun on the lake was skipping over the floor and wall of the porch. The pots of red geraniums and flowered chintz cushions were cheerful in a way nothing had a right to be. The peacefulness was too much for me. All I wanted to do was to destroy the deceptive tranquillity. Mrs. Larimer waited for what I would say.

"What happened to Bryce?"

"You have no right to ask that question." I had never seen her so stern, so angry. I was frightened into silence. "It's not your concern. You created the problem and we had to solve it. You must think of the consequences. My husband and brother simply handled Bryce in the only way they could. Supposing they had called the police? You know how obsessed Bryce was. Before he would have let the police take Matt back to the Beaches he would have killed Matt just as he killed Jess, and then he would have turned the gun on himself. Even if the police had managed to get Matt back alive, which is doubtful, were we to bring Matt back here and then wait day in and day out for Bryce to kidnap him again? The most a court of law would have done was give Bryce a few months in jail. Should we have hired bodyguards for Matt and have him spend the rest of his childhood looking out at the world from a kind of prison?"

"But what did Mr. Larimer and Dr. Bradford do?"

"They did what they had to do. If they had awakened during the night and found someone breaking into our cabin to steal the most precious thing we owned and if that someone had a gun, wouldn't they be justified in taking some kind of action? Bryce had a gun. Do you think he wouldn't have used it?"

"Why are you admitting so much to me? Aren't you afraid I'll go to the police?"

"I don't know what you are imagining, Anne, but I'm admitting nothing to you. And I know you won't go to the police. Think what would happen then. The whole story about Jess's murder would be made public. You may not care about us, but I know you care about Matt. He would never get over it. I'm sure you wouldn't want that on your conscience."

"But they had no right to take the law into their own hands."

"That's simplistic. You're very young. Ten years from now you'll understand the wisdom of what was done— the inevitability of it. Of course you must do what you think right. We can't stop you. But you must also ask yourself how much of this was directly due to your own betrayal of our trust. We hired you to be Matt's keeper. Instead you deceived us, and it was you who allowed all of this to happen to Matt." She got up, carefully folding her needlepoint into a square of clean white cotton to keep it from becoming soiled, and walked into the cabin. Next door I could hear Mrs. Bradford's car driving away.

20

I couldn't find my way out of what had happened. Mrs. Larimer hadn't admitted anything, but what if Bryce had been murdered? Or was I being overly dramatic? Had they merely threatened Bryce? I knew I had to talk to someone, but I didn't know who. I imagined what it would be like for Matt to appear in a witness box and testify against a father who had killed his mother or against a grandfather who had murdered his father. I saw that I couldn't go to the police. The one person I could have talked to at the Beaches, Margot Bradford, was gone. The only thing that kept me sane was the thought that Mrs. Larimer had never really told me what had happened. I let myself believe I had misunderstood, that Bryce was far away, but alive.

The following Friday evening, when the husbands had returned to the Beaches for the weekend and I found out there was to be a meeting, I was sure that somehow the members would discover a way to do what I could not; that they would demand answers and that somehow everything would be made right. I first learned of the meeting at dinner when Syrie said to the children, "They're giving us the van tonight so we can take all of you little brats into Blue Harbor. There's a Disney movie suitable for your innocent eyes."

"Terrific," Meredith said, "but how come?"

"Our betters are having some sort of meeting after supper and they don't want us around. Probably the same old discussion on whether to build up the breakwater."

I guessed immediately what the meeting would be about. While we were watching little animals prancing about in a make-believe forest in a movie, Mr. Larimer and Dr. Bradford would be making their report to the club. They would be telling the members what had happened to Bryce.

After the movie we stopped for ice cream, so it was nearly ten by the time we got back. The only lighted cabin was the Petersons'. Walking along the dark boardwalk, I could feel Matt staying close to me. As we were climbing our porch steps we could hear the members leaving the Petersons' cabin. There were no calls of "Good night" or "See you in the morning," only the sound of doors shutting and the pale glow of the lights going on one by one in the cabins.

Matt was dragging his feet. "What do you think they were talking about at the meeting?" Matt asked.

"Just some club business."

"They were probably talking about me."

"Why do you say that, Matt?"

"Because. I'm nothing but a lot of trouble to everyone. I wish we'd go back to Colonial Gardens."

I tried to reassure Matt, to tell him how much everyone liked him. "You have to put what happened out of your head," I said. I realized with disgust that I was sounding just like the Larimers, telling Matt to forget everything. I wondered how much Matt guessed and hoped it was not much.

At the cabin the Larimers asked Matt a few questions about the movie, but I could see they weren't listening to his answers. "It's way past your bedtime," Mrs. Larimer said to Matt. "Better go upstairs." I waited for them to call me aside and tell me about the meeting, but they went up to their room and closed the door without saying more than good night to me.

It must have been midnight when I heard voices and the sound of a car starting. I got up and looked out my window. The noise was coming from the Parkers' cabin. In the glare of the headlights I could see Mr. Parker getting into the driver's side and the car driving off. The next morning the McKeans left.

At the children's breakfast I expected everyone to be

talking about the sudden departures. "Was someone sick?" I asked.

Syrie shrugged. "That's the Parkers for you. They get an idea and they act on it. I mean right that minute. Mrs. Parker was getting antsy up here. She likes the bright lights."

"But what about the McKeans?"

"They usually go back a little early. They can only stand so much of this togetherness." She changed the subject.

With the Bradfords and the Parkers and the McKeans gone there were only nine families left at the Beaches. The following week the Duncans' grandchildren arrived for two weeks and the Petersons' two children came up with their youngsters so the tables at the children's meals were filled again. Mr. Larimer took a week off from work and stayed at the Beaches. He was wonderful with Matt, gentle and patient. They'd pack a lunch and go out on the Larimers' boat, heading for one of the unoccupied Lake Michigan islands, where they'd explore and picnic. Their relationship had changed in some subtle way: it was less like grandfather and grandson and more like father and son.

August seemed to be rushing by. The bracken was browning and crisping, and along the roadways and around the small lakes in the woods the leaves were turning. The low-slanting sun bathed the paths with a golden light. In the fields the goldenrod and wild asters were in bloom. It might simply have been the season's coming to an end, but there seemed to be a new indolence on the part of the keepers and the children. Tennis and sailing lessons petered out. Everyone went their own way. At the weekend cocktail parties people drifted off into small knots. I was waiting but I didn't know for what. I hadn't told anyone what I believed had happened to Bryce, and day by day the telling seemed more and more impossible.

One afternoon Syrie said, "We're all getting lazy. Mabel promised if we picked enough blackberries she'd make pies for us tonight. So let's go." We followed the path past Grass Lake to a meadow full of blackberry bushes. Protected by jeans and long-sleeved shirts, we gathered the berries. There were cries of "ouch" and hair and shirts to be untangled from thorns. Matt and I were at the edge of the patch. We could see the path deer had made through the briers. The tops of the bushes had been browsed and there were places where the long grass had been crushed. "That's where the deer lay down," I told Matt.

"What if someone came along and shot them?" he wanted to know. He was always asking questions about animals getting hurt, as though everything around him were in danger.

"I think during the hunting season the deer stay in the cedar swamp where it's harder to get to them," I said, hoping to reassure him.

"My granddad used to go into the swamp at night with a flashlight and kill them."

"I didn't think he hunted."

"I mean my granddad Stevens."

"Well, I don't think anyone does that now. Anyhow, shining deer is illegal."

"Was he a crook?"

"I guess he shouldn't have done it. Why don't you talk less and pay more attention to the berries? You're picking ones that aren't ripe."

When we got back to the cabin, I saw a man sitting on the porch with Mrs. Larimer. He waved at me and I returned the wave uncertainly Then I saw it was my father. I was puzzled and surprised. I had been thinking of him as far away in Seattle.

"We've been having a nice talk, Anne," Mrs. Larimer said. "I didn't bore him with all the little problems we've had, but I told him how much we've appreciated your being here this summer." I understood that Mrs. Larimer was warning me not to tell my father anything of what had happened. And then she said something that took me by surprise. "I mentioned to your father that Mr. Larimer and I have been talking about taking the cruiser up to Georgian Bay for the Labor Day weekend. We think it would be a good idea for Matt to get away. We want you to come along to keep an eye on Matt. He's so fond of you. But we'll talk about that later. You two will have a lot to catch up on. Mr. Larimer and I are driving into Blue Harbor to do some errands and we'll take Matt with us. This is Anne's home, Mr. Lewis, and I want you to consider it yours as well. We'd love to have you stay for dinner at the lodge, and we can certainly put you up for the evening."

Dad said, "That's very nice of you, but I have to be off in an hour or two." As soon as the Larimers had left and we were alone I began thinking how I could tell him what had happened, but Dad had his own secret. "I'm sorry I can't stay longer, Annie. I came back because I wanted to tell you and your mother something. I couldn't bring myself to do it over the phone." We were walking along the boardwalk and I could see some of the members looking curiously at us. I didn't know what my dad was going to say, but I had a premonition it would be bad news and I didn't want to hear it with people watching. I steered him toward a path that led into the woods.

"I hope you can understand, Annie. I suppose I seem old to you, but I still have some years ahead of me. The fact is, I'm getting married again. I want you to know I'm going to keep in touch with you and I hope you'll come out and see us." He began to describe his future wife and how well we'd get along, but I had stopped listening. It took all of my effort just to keep from crying.

For a minute I even thought Matt was lucky. His father wanted him so much he kidnapped him. My father had taken off across the country and was issuing a polite invitation for me to drop by sometime and meet his new wife. He might even have a new family. He must have seen the expression on my face, but he misinterpreted it. "Don't worry about your tuition this year. I'm not going to let you down on that. I suppose what you've earned this summer will pay for clothes and books and so forth?" I nodded.

"Now that I've seen the Beaches, I feel a lot better about your being here. It's a little insular, but what a fantastic place to spend the summer! And let an old man give you some advice. If you have a chance to go with the Larimers on their cruiser, do it. My only regrets are all the things I could have done and didn't because I took my responsibilities too seriously."

His "responsibilities." That was another word for my mother and me. Evidently he felt we had stood in the way of what he *really* wanted to do. I longed to tell him what had happened, to retaliate by shouting out to him that the cabin he admired was the home of a murderer. That the Beaches was a sham. But he wouldn't want to know. He was on the way to leaving his "responsibilities" behind him. I felt betrayed. He was going to start a glorious new life and the last thing he would want to hear about would be his daughter's problems. He was going to be free in some new way he couldn't name. He was as foolish as I was.

Instead I showed him around the club property—the lodge and the tennis courts and the beach. Everywhere we went there were people to introduce him to: keepers with their charges, the club members, Mabel and Lyle and Thomas. Everyone went out of their way to be pleasant to him except Thomas, who seemed to suggest by the way he said "So that's your father" that he wasn't impressed.

By the end of the afternoon I saw that it was hard for

my father to say good-bye to me. However much he was looking forward to some bright new future, he was sorry to leave me behind. He did care for me. But by then we were standing by his car and several of the club members were nearby. It was too late to tell him what had happened. I was thankful the members were there. Left to ourselves, I think we both would have cried.

Matt had watched me say good-bye to my father. When Dad was gone Matt came over and pulled at my arm in an affectionate way. "Come on in the cabin," he said. "I'll make you some popcorn. *The Empire Strikes Back* is on the Movie Channel. Things are better in outer space."

21

I had been too preoccupied with my father to think about the Larimers' surprising offer to go on their boat with them, but Mrs. Larimer mentioned it again after dinner. Matt and Lance were inside watching *Dr. No* and I had been sitting on the porch trying to think what I could write my mother. Whatever their differences were, I knew she still loved my father. His marriage would be devastating for her. I knew something else. If I had had thoughts of confiding in my mother about what had happened at the Beaches, of asking her advice, I could forget them now. It wasn't the time to inflict my own problems on her. She would have all she could do to get used to the idea of Dad married again.

I was so thoroughly back in Colonial Gardens with my mother, I didn't notice Mrs. Larimer standing in the doorway. "Do you mind if I sit out here with you?" she said. "The television set is driving me wild."

"No, I'd be glad for the company." It was true. I had come to the end of my speculation on my parents and I was going over and over the same miserable conclusion—that nothing would ever be the way it was.

"I'm sorry about your parents, Anne. Your father seems like a very nice man." I think she was going to say something about the divorce but sensed it was the last thing I wanted to talk about. Instead she said, "You must have been a little startled when I mentioned the trip to Georgian Bay but Mr. Larimer and I feel it would be good for all of us to have a change of scene."

"It sounds great," I said. "I've never seen that country, but I should really go home. I think my mother might need me."

Before she could mask her feelings I saw how disappointed Mrs. Larimer was. None of this was suggested in her answer. "Take all the time you like to think it over, Anne, but remember we think of you as a member of the family now. We'd hate to go without you. Matt has grown attached to you and nothing is more important for him now than consistent relationships; he's lost so much this past year. We have a week before Labor Day. Take a few days to think about it." Her voice had faltered when she mentioned Labor Day. On that weekend it would be exactly a year since Jess died. She had tears in her eyes. No wonder they wanted to get away. She got up. "I'll just go and see how the boys are coming along."

I wasn't sure what the Larimers were offering me. The talk of traveling together with Mrs. Larimer and Matt suggested I was to be something more than a keeper. It was almost as though they wanted me to take Jess's place. Even the timing was appropriate, for that was the weekend they had lost her. It was a seductive idea, especially with my own family falling apart.

But something warned me to be cautious. The Beaches was like a primitive tribe into which you were initiated and to which you belonged forever. I remembered reading about some explorers in the Philippines who believed they had discovered a tribe untouched by civilization. Later they found it was a hoax. Under clothes fashioned from bark and leaves were stylish shorts and brassieres. A little distance from the caves the tribe was thought to live in were furnished shacks where the tribe went when the explorers were gone. The Beaches was like that—only just the opposite. When the outside world was watching them the members were civilized, cultured, elegant, but behind that facade they were as primitive as any savage tribe.

In the warm August evening I was chilled by these thoughts. I saw what my choices were. I could join the tribe and receive all the gifts they had to offer. The circle would close around me and I would be protected. Or I could threaten to tell the truth about what had happened. Then I would be an enemy of the tribe, a danger to them. Would they hunt me down just as they hunted Bryce down? Had they been capable of murder once? And if they had, with so much at stake, would they be capable of it again?

The trip on their boat suddenly seemed dangerous, the out-of-the-way places Mr. Larimer might take us menacing. I thought, I'm becoming paranoid, crazy. I had to talk to Ed. I started to go into the cabin to use the phone but a sudden feeling of caution warned me not to. Instead I walked over to the lodge to use the phone there. The lodge was empty. The tables in the dining room were set for the children's breakfast and Mabel and the rest of the kitchen staff were gone. An ashtray was filled with cigarette stubs and someone had left newspapers and a pink sweater on the leather couch. Tacked to the bulletin board was a notice of the final tennis tournament. It all seemed so commonplace, so ordinary. I began to have second thoughts. Were all the bad things that had happened delusions? Still I went to the phone and called Ed. The following day would be Sunday, the keepers' day off.

I was so relieved to hear Ed's voice I could hardly answer him. "Hey," he said, "where are you? You sound a million miles away."

"I'm right here at the Beaches. I want to see you."

"Well, I'm really in demand these days, but I guess I could spare a little time for an old friend. Like right now." He sounded pleased, even eager.

"Could we get together tomorrow? It's Sunday and I'll have the afternoon off. I think I could use the Larimers' station wagon to come over to Lakeville."

"I could come to the Beaches."

"No, it's better if I meet you."

"You sound mysterious. Are some of those old goats trying to make out with you?"

"I just have to talk."

Ed stopped joking. "Okay. Whatever time you want to come. Meet me in beautiful downtown Lakeville at our hardware store. The store will be closed but I'll get the key. And Annie, I'm glad you called."

As I was hanging up I heard someone behind me. It was Mr. Peterson.

"Sorry to disturb you, Anne," he said. "Just wanted to snitch this copy of *The Wall Steet Journal.* Don't tell on me." He picked up the paper and walked off toward his cabin.

22

On Sunday afternoons at the Beaches life seemed to stop. The newspapers had been read, the tennis courts and beaches were empty, the men returning to the city were already on their way. The members left behind sat with unopened books on their laps or languished on their porches. Later some of the women would get up a bridge game and a few of the keepers, free of their charges, would wander over to the croquet court. The children, who were so noisy and conspicuous during the week, were hidden away playing at secret things behind closed doors.

I found Mrs. Larimer making a halfhearted attempt to organize some photographs in an album. I didn't want to mention Lakeville and Ed, so I asked if I could take the station wagon up to Blue Harbor. "Of course you're welcome to the station wagon, Anne, but the stores are all closed on Sunday, aren't they?" she asked.

"I think the drugstore is open and I'm out of things to read."

"This house is full of books. Just help yourself. No need to drive all that way."

"You don't have anything trashy enough," I said, trying to make my voice light. "What I really want is a fast read."

"I'm afraid the club has been a bad influence. You were much more discriminating when you first came. Didn't I see some volumes of Dickens in your room?"

I hadn't known she had been in my room, and the books were in my suitcase. "If you would rather I didn't take the wagon . . . ," I said.

Immediately she was reassuring. "No, please take it. I just thought I might spare you the trip, but I don't blame you for wanting to get away, even to Blue Harbor. No place in the world is as dull as the Beaches on a Sunday afternoon."

The streets in Lakeville were deserted but about a block from the hardware store I saw Mr. Peterson's maroon Lincoln in my rearview mirror. As he passed me Mr. Peterson slowed down and waved. I was too startled to wave back. Instead I drove past the store and up the first street I came to, parking in front of a neat little white cottage with window boxes filled with petunias and ivy. As I stopped to lock the station wagon I could hear music from a radio or television. A choir was singing a hymn I recalled from my childhood. I had a crazy desire to bang on the door of the house and like a fleeing refugee ask for asylum. Instead I made myself walk slowly toward the main street. I waited to be sure Mr. Peterson's car was gone and then I went quickly to the front door of the hardware store where Ed had been watching for me.

"What's going on? I saw you drive past the store."

"I was trying to get away from Mr. Peterson."

"Hays Peterson? I wouldn't have thought little girls were his thing."

I was looking around at the shelves neatly stacked with boxes of nails and bolts, tools, light bulbs, hoses, pots and pans. It was incredible how many needs a store like that could meet.

Ed watched me. "Can I sell you an extension cord or some ready-mix cement? Is that what you came for, just to get me back here where I work all week? Annie, what's the matter with you?"

He put his arms around me. I rested my head on his shoulder for a moment and then I pulled away. "Is there a back room?" I asked.

"A back room? We've got a john we could squeeze into. What do you have in mind?"

"Stop being funny, Ed. I have to tell you something awful and I don't want anyone to look through the windows and see me here."

"I was just teasing you. Dad's got a little office. We can go in there."

I followed him into a room not much larger than a good-sized closet. There was a small table that served as a desk, a bookcase filled with ledgers and sample books, and a couple of chairs. On the walls were old pictures of high school football and baseball teams, an out-of-date calendar from a paint company, and a photograph of Ed with what I guessed were his brother and sisters and a large black dog that was like a blot of ink on the picture. "What's the dog's name?" I asked.

"Annie, save the small talk and tell me what's bothering you."

"It's the Beaches. It's not what it seems. I'm sure Mr. Peterson followed me here because I know they've killed Bryce."

Ed stared at me. "Look, that's bizarre. Let's start with Peterson. What makes you think he's following you?"

"He overheard me call you last night, and what else would he be doing in Lakeville on a Sunday?"

"Ford Baker, who is a resident of this town, even on Sundays, is enlarging Peterson's garage at the Beaches and making a screen porch for him. Peterson has stopped by Baker's place several times to leave off plans or to talk things over with Baker. Peterson comes into the hardware store all the time. The man's obsessive about the way he wants the addition done. And now about Bryce, he's not dead. The creep he was living with was in here the other day with a letter from California sent by Bryce."

His voice hardened when he mentioned Bryce's name. I realized he was jealous of Bryce, of the way I kept talking about him. But I couldn't help myself. "How do you know it was from Bryce?" I asked. "Mr. Larimer's company has offices all over. He could have arranged to have it sent."

Too late I saw my mistake. I had been wanting to tell my story for such a long time that I had just blurted it out without giving any thought to how it might sound to Ed. Instead of leading Ed step by step through the whole thing, I had started with Bryce. Now everything I said would be suspect. My outburst made me sound unhinged. I knew Ed liked me, more than liked me, but now I saw his interest in me change. He wouldn't want to have anything to do with a lunatic like me. I tried to begin at the beginning, describing my first meeting with Bryce.

"Look," Ed said, "I guessed something was going on between you and Bryce, but whatever it was, I'd just as soon not hear about it. I mean, I'm not boring you with stories about my girlfriends. Anyhow, I thought the Larimers didn't want Matt seeing his father, so how come you let him? I mean, you were supposed to be Matt's *keeper*." He was angry over my seeing Bryce.

I thought that at least there was something I could do to ease my conscience, so I said, "I just want you to know that Robin didn't destroy those orchids. Bryce did that."

Ed flushed. "Nice boyfriends you have. You took long enough to clear Robin. A week before Labor Day is a little late to write the Grub and tell him all is forgiven and he can forget about his exile in camp."

"I guess I'd better get back," I said.

"I think you should," Ed said. "The Beaches is certainly where you belong."

23

Though Eagletown was halfway between Lakeville and the Beaches, the Indian town was seldom mentioned at the club. It was just a place you drove through on the way to Lakeville or Blue Harbor. All I knew about it was that Thomas and some of his relatives lived there. The houses were small and cramped looking, houses where people got on each other's nerves, houses where there were few secrets. You could tell from the wash hanging out on lines that at least some of the families couldn't afford dryers. The cars in the driveways were old and rusted. Farther up the shore was a larger reservation, Duck Lake. The tribe that lived there had opened a successful gambling casino and its members were prospering, although there was some talk that the alcohol the casino served was becoming a problem for younger tribe members; there was more money but more of it was being spent on drink. None of that prosperity was visible in Eagletown, although I was sure that at least Thomas was well paid by the Beaches. As I drove by on my way back to the Beaches I tried to guess which house was his, but no one house looked more prosperous than another.

Because I was busy studying the houses, I didn't notice a dog running out into the road until it was nearly under my tires. I swerved and slammed on the brakes, just missing it. I had been upset after my talk with Ed and the near accident left me so shaky I pulled over to the curb and stopped the car. The squeal of my brakes brought people to their windows and front porches. They stared silently at me for a few moments and then turned away. Two small children ran over to round up the dog and take it back into a house.

A man stood outside watching me. It was Thomas. We looked at each other and then he walked across the bare yards and over to my car. He must have seen at once how upset I was, because he said, "You want me to drive you back?"

"No, I'll be fine. It was just such a close call."

He said, "Come in my house and I'll give you a cup of coffee." I didn't want to go back to the Beaches and I was curious to see where Thomas lived. "Move over," he directed, "and I'll pull the car in my driveway."

Thomas's small house had white clapboard siding but

inside I was surprised to see it was a log cabin. "It was my daddy's place," Thomas said. "I fixed up the outside."

"Who lives with you, Thomas?" I asked. I realized I didn't even know if he had a family.

"My wife died six years ago. One of my boys went to the city. I told him it wasn't a good idea but he didn't listen. Most of the time he doesn't work." Thomas's face brightened. "But his son, my grandson, I'm sending him to college. He's going to be a teacher. My other boy married a girl over in Duck Lake. He's got a job at the restaurant next to the casino."

"You live all by yourself?"

"I got the tribe."

Apart from the fragrance of sweet grass there was nothing in the house to suggest it was the home of an Indian. I don't know what I expected—animal skins on the wall, a tomahawk or a peace pipe on the table. While Thomas was in the kitchen making coffee, I looked around the room. There was a television set and opposite it a large, worn lounge chair. Some of the tables and chairs had a rustic twenties look and I decided they must have been castoffs from the Beaches. Old magazines, ones I recognized from the club, were piled up beside the lounge chair. A new refrigerator, evidently too large for the small kitchen, stood against a living room wall. On one of the tables were some snapshots of what I took to be Thomas's sons. They were wearing blue jeans and work shirts and one of the boys had his hair in a ponytail. There was also a picture of a boy about high school age dressed in his graduation cap and gown.

Thomas put the coffee cups down on a table and eased himself into the lounge chair.

"Thomas, aren't you afraid to keep working at the Beaches?"

"Where else would I work? Anyhow, why should I be afraid?"

"You know everything about them—what happened to Jess and Bryce. I think Mr. Peterson has been following me around and you know lots more than I do."

"I don't know anything about what went on when they found Matt and Bryce and you don't either. Anyhow, whatever I think about them, the club knows I'm not going to say anything. What I do is between me and my own tribe. What happens to them is up to their people to decide."

"I don't know what to do."

"You could go home," Thomas said.

"I'm worried about leaving Matt."

"Maybe, but you're more worried about pleasing yourself. The Beaches is a comfortable place to stay."

I was hurt by what he said because there was so much truth in it. "You'll never say anything?" I asked.

He was sipping his coffee in a way that made me see he was an expert in enjoying small things; he wouldn't waste time waiting for larger pleasures he did not expect. "Like I say, it's not my tribe."

"But they're part of your life." I indicated the furniture and the magazines.

"Some of their things come my way, but I don't need them. I don't need things the way they do. They couldn't live without their things. If you turned me out in the woods right now I could make out. If you turned them out the first thing they'd say is, 'Where is Thomas?' They just float around out there. I'm their connection with the earth. They have to have me. I don't have to have them. Anyhow, that land is getting away from them. In a few more years it's going to be all sand and water."

"That's what Bryce said." But I felt there was a difference: Bryce wanted the land taken from the Beaches as a punishment. Thomas didn't care one way or another; it was up to the land. "You were good to Matt, you must care about him."

"He belongs to them now. They bought him just like they're buying you."

I drove slowly back toward the Beaches thinking that in one way or another I had made it impossible for myself to tell the truth. I had let Mrs. Bradford leave without saying anything. I hadn't confided in either my mother or father and now I had made Ed so angry he wouldn't believe anything I told him. Both Ed and Thomas knew me better than I knew myself. I decided I had to leave the Beaches, but I didn't believe the Larimers would let me.

24

As Labor Day drew closer the amount of activity at the club increased. Screens were pulled down, windows boarded up, and station wagons packed. The Clementses and the Brightmans left to a chorus of "See you next summer." Mrs. Larimer tried to reassure Matt, who stood in the roadway watching the Brightmans' departing car. "When we get back to the city, you'll have a chance to see Lance," she said. "For now, why don't you and Anne go for a walk while I try to get the rest of our things packed. Did you keep out the clothes you'll need for the boat trip like I told you to?"

"They're on my bed," Matt said. "Where are you going to put the toad?"

"Are you absolutely sure you want to take that poor creature to the city? It would be much better off if you would just let it go." She saw Matt's face. "All right, we'll find a place for it. Now just get out from underfoot. Oh, Anne, did you let your mother know you were going with us to Georgian Bay?"

"I wrote her yesterday." It had been four days since I had talked to Ed and Thomas. Twice during those four days I had asked to use the station wagon and each time Mrs. Larimer had some excuse for not letting me have it. Now I was never alone at the Beaches. When I went to the lodge to use the phone, someone always seemed to be there. Mrs. Larimer had taken to carrying our outgoing mail to the club box at the entrance to the property and always asked if I had something to mail. She saw all my letters. Even on walks in the woods with Matt a member of the club turned up. If I felt like a prisoner at the Beaches, I could imagine what it would be like on the Larimers' cruiser. I began to make plans.

The Labor Day weekend meant breaks in the usual routine. On one evening the adults and children had dinner together. After dessert everyone sang, "Come in, come in, come in, dear Mabel, come in, come in." As Mabel appeared in the kitchen doorway everyone applauded, and Mr. Peterson made a gracious speech about the quality of her cooking and how the children would miss her cookies and he would miss her famous German chocolate cake. Mabel blushed and said something about it being a privilege to cook for such an appreciative group and that she would be practicing new recipes ("receipts," she called them) over the winter and would be ready when Memorial Day came. She told Mr. Peterson she would make his favorite cake and send it over for our supper the following evening, which in keeping with the Beaches' tradition would be a picnic on the beach and the final bonfire of the season. On the way out several of the members stopped to thank Mabel. I managed to be the last. When we were alone for a moment I slipped a sealed envelope into her apron pocket. "Could you give that letter to Ed when you get back to Lakeville?" I whispered. "It's important, but don't mention it to anyone else."

Her face brightened. She thought she was encouraging a romance. "Don't worry. I'll drop it off."

After dinner Matt said, "I want to go fishing one more time." We wandered down to the landing and Matt put his fly rod together and began casting into the current. Desperately wanting to land a trout, he hardly breathed as the fly floated downstream. There were already a few red leaves floating in the current from trees that were beginning to turn. We had only been at the landing a few minutes when Mr. Stockton arrived with his waders. "Hope I'm not disturbing you kids. I just wanted to get a half hour or so of fishing in before I have to pack up my gear. Say, Matt, you're developing into a pretty competent fisherman."

Matt was disappointed. He had wanted the river for

himself. After a short time he gave up and we left the stream to Mr. Stockton. Matt said in a disgusted voice, "You can't move in this place without someone breathing down your neck." I had not been surprised to see Mr. Stockton. I was sure someone would follow us there, but I didn't know if they were keeping an eye on me or on Matt.

The next afternoon I packed my suitcase, knowing I would leave it behind. I had a large beach bag I planned to take to the bonfire later that evening, and I crammed all the things I valued and wanted to take with me into it—my best sweater, photographs of Matt and Ed taken during the summer, my letters from home. I tried to stay away from the Larimers, afraid they would see how nervous I was, but it was getting dark and I knew I would have to go down to the beach for the bonfire. I slung the beach bag over my shoulder. Several people carried them to hold blankets and insect repellent.

I was afraid I would never see Matt again. I put an arm around his shoulder and for once he didn't shake it off. I wondered if he sensed something, but he only said, "I don't know if I'll ever come back here again, Annie, but if I do I hope you'll be my keeper." Then, embarrassed by what he had said, he ran on ahead of me. Matt's trust almost made me decide to stay. I didn't want to desert him. But as soon as I drew near to the club members and felt their surreptitious scrutiny of me, I knew that in spite of Matt I had to escape.

Matt and I settled next to the Larimers, who were

describing the trip to Georgian Bay to the Clementses. "That's still God's country," Mr. Larimer said. "You can travel for hours on the boat without seeing a soul."

I waited until it was nearly dark and then I got up as though I were going to join Syrie, who was sitting at the edge of the bonfire. In a minute I was away from the beach and in the shadows of the trees. In another minute I was running down the road that led to the club entrance.

Ed was waiting. I pulled open the van door and climbed in. "Mabel gave me your message. I think she believed we were eloping," Ed said. "At first I wasn't going to come. I thought we had said our good-byes, but the note sounded desperate."

He still hadn't forgiven me for Robin and for Bryce. "You've saved my life, literally," I said. "Please, Ed, if you'll just drive me to Blue Harbor, I can make the bus that comes from Mackinaw City; it will take me downstate."

"I don't understand. What's the hurry?"

"I'm supposed to leave tomorrow with Matt and the Larimers on their boat for a trip to Georgian Bay."

"Lucky you."

"No, you don't understand. They don't trust me. They'll find a way to get rid of me on the trip like they got rid of Bryce."

"You still believe that crap about their doing something to Bryce? That's bad enough, but to think they would do something to you is absolutely paranoid. Annie, you're sick and the best thing I can do for you is not to put you on some bus to God knows where but to get some help for you." Ed started up the van and turned into the road that led to the Beaches.

"Where are you going?"

"I'm going to take you to the Larimers and tell them what you told me. They're responsible for you while you're here, and they ought to know just how far out you are."

When the van slowed for a sharp curve in the road, I opened the door and jumped out. I heard Ed calling me but I ran through the trees back toward the main road. When I reached the road I hid in the shadows, hoping someone might come along and I could hitch a ride. I saw a car leave the Beaches. There hadn't been time for Ed to get to the club members and for them to send someone to find me. I thought Ed might have changed his mind and was coming back for me after all, but it wasn't Ed's car. It was Thomas's pickup. Impulsively I ran out onto the road and Thomas braked his truck.

He leaned across the front seat, opening the door for me. "What the hell are you doing out here? Looks like you can't keep out of trouble."

"Thomas, I've got to get away. Can you take me into Blue Harbor? I want to catch the bus home."

"Sure. I've been telling you to go back home, haven't I? You've finally had enough of the Beaches, eh? I saw your boyfriend coming in the road while I was going out. You sure you didn't just have a lovers' quarrel and that's why you're running away?" He studied his rear-view mirror. "It looks like Ed might be coming after you."

I turned around and saw the headlights of a car gaining on us. "I don't think it's Ed. I think it's someone from the Beaches. Please don't give me away. I don't want to go back."

"You're a big girl. You can do what you want to."

"I think Ed told them something to make them want to bring me back. Please, isn't there some way I could hide?"

Thomas smiled. "I never have any trouble fooling them. You slip down off the seat onto the floor and I'll throw my jacket over you." In a minute the car behind us, which was traveling much faster than we were, caught up with Thomas's truck and honked several times. Thomas pulled over and cranked open his window. "What's the matter?"

I was wedged between the seat and the front of the truck, hidden under Thomas's jacket. The rough wool covered my face and I breathed in the smell of tobacco and wood smoke. I recognized Mr. Larimer's voice, off-hand but insistent. "Did you pass Anne Lewis anywhere?"

"Is she in the station wagon?"

"No, she's not in any car. She was walking."

"This time of night? What's the matter with that girl? No, I haven't seen anyone except Ed. He nearly slammed into me when I was coming out."

"Sorry. I think he was a little frantic. He and Anne

had some sort of quarrel and she took off. We want to find her before something happens to her. Could you come back and give us a hand? She might be in the woods."

"Wish I could but I promised I'd help my cousin Danny put some fishnets out tonight. He wants to get them in before the big holiday crowd gets out there in their boats. Sorry."

"That's all right. If you do see Anne, I'd appreciate it if you'd get in touch with us right away. I'm afraid she's pretty upset." I heard Mr. Larimer's car speed away. Thomas was chuckling.

The bus stop was in a gas station on the edge of town. Because it was the end of the holiday weekend, several people were lined up on the benches in front of the station. At first the clerk didn't want to sell me a ticket. "No seats left," he said. I told him I didn't care, that I'd stand all the way. He gave me a funny look, as though I were too anxious. I must not have looked dangerous, because after a moment he relented. "Well, you won't have to do that," he said. "A passenger from Mackinaw City is getting off a little way south of here. I shouldn't, but I'll sell you that seat."

Thomas offered to wait with me for the bus. "Thanks, but if anyone is looking for me your truck will attract their attention. You're supposed to be in Eagletown setting out your fishnets." I took his hand. He looked embarrassed and in a minute he was driving away without looking back. I stayed in the service station studying the soft-drink machine, trying to look as though I were deciding what I wanted to drink. It was only minutes before the bus arrived.

I had planned to go to the police when I got back to the city, but in the darkness of the bus I began to be unsure of what I would tell them. Hadn't Jess hit her head? Technically Bryce had not killed her. And Ed said Bryce was out in California. Would they think, like Ed, that I was crazy? Certainly the Larimers would suggest that. It would be my word against theirs and they were an important part of the community. And even more important, what would a police investigation mean for Matt? I knew I wouldn't say anything. But as relieved as I had been to escape, I already missed the Beaches. I began to wonder if I had been foolish. I saw the members as they would have been at that moment, walking back to their cabins carrying their candles. I remembered Mrs. Larimer's arm around me. I would never be able to see Matt again. I was cast out. I didn't know whether I had saved my life or lost it.

Seeing the lake and the beach, the woods and the cabins after three years brings it all back. And I try for the thousandth time to sort out what really happened.

When I returned to the city I wrote to Ed to ask if anyone had heard from Bryce, but there was no answer to my letter. For a while I used to drive down the Larimers' street, hoping to catch a glimpse of Matt. One evening a police car stopped me and the officers inside ordered me not to come there again. They accused me of "harassing" the Larimers.

Mother and I gave up our home in Colonial Gardens and moved to an apartment in the city. I finished college and found a job I like and I've made some good friends, but I still think of the Beaches. And I miss Matt. Most of the time I believe I did the right thing in running away, yet there are days when I believe I was foolish. I see myself on the Larimers' boat on the way to Georgian Bay. There is nothing to do but sit on the deck in the sunshine, watching the blue water around us and the gulls over us. Matt and the Larimers are on the deck with me. We are laughing over the funny things we remember from the summer at the Beaches and already making plans for the summer to come. Or I see myself at night in a storm. Matt is taken below by his grandmother. In the face of the storm Mr. Larimer gives me some task that requires me to stay on deck. The boat heaves through mammoth waves. I imagine the slippery deck, the lurching and pitching and then some sudden attack—I am never sure from whom it comes. I hear Mr. Larimer's belated shout to his wife and Matt to come quickly, that Anne has been washed overboard. Then I feel the water closing over me.

I wonder if the Beaches has been judged, and like plagues, the water and the sand have been sent to drive the club members away. Their cabins will be torn down to make a park. In a few years the sand will cover the foundations of the cabins like forgetfulness. The wood lilies and windflowers will spread across the encroaching sand like forgiveness.